Mennyms Under Siege

SYLVIA WAUGH was for twenty years a teacher of English literature. She always wanted to write, but *The Mennyms,* her first book, was not written until after her retirement. It was received with acclaim on both sides of the Atlantic. She lives in England with her husband and three grown children and is at work on the next book in the Mennyms series.

Mennyms Under Siege

SYLVIA WAUGH

AN AVON CAMELOT BOOK

AVON BOOKS
A division of
The Hearst Corporation
1350 Avenue of the Americas
New York, New York 10019

Copyright © 1995 by Sylvia Waugh
Published by arrangement with William Morrow and Company, Inc.
Library of Congress Catalog Card Number: 95-1500
ISBN: 0-380-72584-3
RL: 6.0

First Avon Camelot Printing: March 1997

CAMELOT TRADEMARK REG. U.S. PAT. OFF. AND IN OTHER COUNTRIES, MARCA REGISTRADA,
HECHO EN U.S.A.

Printed in the U.S.A.

OPM   10 9 8 7 6 5 4 3 2 1

For Julia, my publisher,
who gave me great encouragement.
And for Karen,
who gave me good advice.

. . . Life piled on life
Were all too little, and of one to me
Little remains; but every hour is saved
From that eternal silence, something more,
A bringer of new things . . .

Ulysses Tennyson

Contents

1

Bangs

"I need bangs."

Pilbeam was gazing at herself critically in a mirror propped up on the kitchen table. Her long black hair was combed back from her broad forehead. Her mother, busy ironing, looked up from her work and smiled.

"Need? Surely you mean 'want' or 'would like'?"

"No," said Pilbeam. "I do mean need."

Vinetta stood the iron on its heel and went and sat down beside her eldest daughter.

"Well, come on. Explain yourself," she said. "It's not like you to use the word 'need' so carelessly."

"I need bangs," said Pilbeam, "to hide my brow and to act as a sort of disguise for the outside world."

That was a fair enough reason, but obviously not the complete story.

"You've managed well enough so far," said her mother. "What is different now?"

"I want to go to the theater," said Pilbeam. "Really go to a real theater. I will be sitting next to *people*. I need my face to be as veiled as possible by my hair."

Her hair reached nearly to her waist. It was thick and

1

heavy and looked completely genuine. Pilbeam was the family beauty, like the princess out of a fairytale. And the Mennyms were a strange family, a family of life-sized rag dolls created forty-four years before by Kate Penshaw, a lonely old lady whose hobby became her passion in life. After her death, the dolls had come mysteriously to life and taken over Number 5 Brocklehurst Grove, living there almost as if they were human. Except for Pilbeam. She was the last of Kate's creations and had lain unfinished in the attic for forty years. Soobie, her twin, had found her in a wicker chest and Vinetta, her loving mother, had finished the work that Kate had long ago begun.

The taking over of Kate's house had been surprisingly easy. Her heir, Chesney Loftus, had failed to come from Australia to claim, or even inspect, his inheritance. Among Kate's papers the Mennyms had found the name of an agent to whom they had written claiming to have been Kate's paying guests, and asking to be allowed to remain on as tenants of the property. Chesney himself had died three years ago, leaving the house he had never seen to what he must have assumed to be his aging tenants, for however long Sir Magnus and/or his son Joshua should reside there. He would clearly not have expected them to live forever. On their demise, the property was to go to an English branch of Kate's family.

In the forty-four years of their residence, the Mennyms had never found it difficult to come and go to the shops and the market and the park. It was simply a matter of wearing clothes to cover cloth, and dark glasses of various styles to hide button eyes. But this going to a theater was different. How different, Vinetta was not sure. She was startled at the thought of her daughter being in such close proximity to people, but she respected Pilbeam's wishes and trusted her judgment. It was her deeply held belief that one should not be constantly frustrating the young.

She looked closely at Pilbeam's hairline.

"If I combed your hair forward," she said, "I suppose I could cut some of it into bangs for you."

"No," said Pilbeam, "that wouldn't do. It might make a line across the top and it would thin the hair down. I want more hair on top, not less. You could try making bangs and stitching them into place. Then if ever I didn't want them we could unpick them, like Dad's beard when he was Santa Claus at Peachum's."

"What would I use to make them?" said Vinetta. "Your hair is so beautiful and silky. It would have to be an exact match. There's nothing suitable in my workbox. I know there's not."

"No problem," said her daughter. "Just cut a few inches off the bottom. I have often thought it was a bit too long at the back."

The transplant was performed that very afternoon. Poopie and Wimpey, the ten-year-old twins, came and watched, fascinated. It was a frosty January day with lowering clouds threatening snow. The twins were bored enough to welcome the distraction of seeing their elder sister suffer. It was not painful, of course, just irritating and restricting. Pilbeam was not at all pleased that her two younger siblings were such earnest spectators.

"It must feel funny," said Wimpey as she watched the needle going in and out on Pilbeam's brow. She stood with her head on one side, looking up at her mother and sister. Wimpey's pale blue button eyes were always full of wonder. Her golden curls, tied in bunches with satin ribbon, made her look old-fashioned and even more doll-like than the rest of them.

"Hold still," said Vinetta when Pilbeam turned her head to look at her sister. "I don't want to get the thread in a tangle."

Joshua, their father, coming into the kitchen after his nap, raised his eyebrows and then took refuge in the brown teapot, pretending to brew tea in it and pour it out into his old mug. He was a quiet man, his dollness well hidden beneath a gruff manner. Like all the family, his life was a mixture of reality and pretence. He really did work as a nightwatchman at Sydenham's Warehouse. He really did tend the garden at home, helped by his son Poopie. But the pipe he "smoked" was a pretend. The "tea" he brewed was make-believe. There really is a football team called Port Vale, one of the oldest in the English League, but Joshua, their lifelong supporter, had never been to see them play.

When she had finished fixing the bangs in place, Vinetta stood back to admire her work. Then she held one mirror in front of Pilbeam and another behind to let her daughter see her hair from every angle. The twins watched her.

Poopie looked up from under his own yellow bangs, cut straight across his brow, bright blue eyes glinting. "I don't like you with bangs," he said. "I liked you better before."

Pilbeam looked at herself anxiously.

4

"What do you think, Dad?" she asked Joshua.

"Not much different," said her father, barely raising his eyes from the newspaper he had begun to read.

"Well, I think it looks lovely," said Wimpey.

Miss Quigley came in to collect a bottle for Googles, the baby. For the past three years, she had been nanny to Vinetta's youngest child. Before that she had "lived" in the hall cupboard, appearing in the Mennym house at intervals as a visitor and Vinetta's friend. Her own home was supposed to be in Trevethick Street, but that was just a pretend. She was a lady of uncertain age with a plain but pleasant face and thin hair tied in a tight little bun on the back of her neck. Since moving properly into the house, she had developed talents, not only as a nanny but also as an artist painting pictures that, had she been human and not a rag doll, would surely have led to her work receiving wide acclaim. She took one look at Pilbeam and smiled a tight little smile.

"Snow White has turned into Cleopatra," she said as she passed by.

Pilbeam looked annoyed, and Vinetta, seeing the expression on her daughter's face, knew just what was coming next.

"It must look odd," said Pilbeam. "We'll have to unpick it."

"Take your time," said her mother. "Think about it. Get used to it. Remember, it was your idea in the first place. And you did say you *needed* bangs."

Vinetta was reluctant that her work of the past two hours should be completely wasted. She wished dear Hortensia had been a little more tactful. It was nothing to say really, no insult to be likened to the Queen of Egypt, but young people do take things so seriously. Pilbeam suited her new hairstyle. Anyone with any taste could see that. And after a day or two they all did.

"It makes you look older," said Granny Tulip. "More grown up."

"I *am* more grown up," said Pilbeam.

It was Tuesday, and she and Tulip and Vinetta were sitting in the breakfast-room, which was Tulip's office in this house that was home to three generations. Lady Tulip Mennym was an amazing woman. With her white hair and her blue-checked apron, she looked a typical, housewifely granny. She was small and neat and quick in speech and movement. But in addition to this, she was an excellent businesswoman. And, as if that were not enough, she was so skilled at knitting that the most famous store in London sold the garments she designed and made. Harrods, naturally, was never aware that the firm of 'tulipmennym' was so different from any of their other suppliers.

There was something in the tone of Pilbeam's voice that made her grandmother look up, shrewd crystal eyes showing an awareness that Pilbeam was making a real statement and not just uttering empty words.

"In fact," Pilbeam went on, "I have decided to be eighteen instead of sixteen. Soobie agrees. Since last year, we have moved on. The whole family has. But, in our case, it meant more. We were adolescents. Now we are grown up."

Vinetta said anxiously, "Eighteen or sixteen—there's little difference. We are as we are. And, whether we like it or not, our circle is complete. In the human world, change is constant. Children grow up and get married and grow old. That sort of cycle is not possible for us. We wouldn't want it anyway. We do well enough as we are. In more than forty years we have never grown any older. There are many in the world outside this house who would envy us.''

It was less than a month since their one and only contact with a human being had been finally severed. Albert Pond, Kate Penshaw's great-nephew, had been called upon by the ghost of Kate to save the Mennym family when their home at Number 5 Brocklehurst Grove had been threatened with demolition to make room for a motorway. With the exception of Sir Magnus, everyone in the family came to look on Albert Pond as one of themselves, an honorary rag doll, but his departure became essential when he seemed to be falling in love with Pilbeam, and she with him.

Pilbeam smiled at her mother, poor, worried Vinetta, whose sensibilities made it difficult for her to find the right words.

''It's all right, Mum,'' said Pilbeam. ''I know I'll never have a boyfriend. I don't think Granny could knit me one! Growing up, being mature, means accepting what you are and making the most of it. Soobie has changed too, you know, Mother. He has learned to enjoy life more, even as a blue rag doll, jogging secretly through the dark streets. Maybe it's the tracksuit that's done it!''

Soobie, Pilbeam's twin, was unlike every other member of the family, for he was completely blue from head to foot and his eyes were bright, shining, intelligent silver buttons.

Vinetta looked pleased at Pilbeam's words about the

tracksuit. Vinetta had bought it at Peachum's, the town's biggest department store, when Soobie's old, striped blue linen suit was in tatters and he had at last agreed to wear a more modern, more human, style of clothing.

"I think you're right," said Vinetta. "Soobie really does look smart in a tracksuit."

Pilbeam laughed.

"That was a joke, Mum. Why do you always have to take everything so literally?"

Vinetta smiled.

"Part of my nature, I suppose. I am a bit too set in my ways to move on very far."

"Well, I'm not," said Pilbeam. "So take it as a fact. I am eighteen years old. And so is Soobie. We are not children."

"Where does that leave Appleby?" asked Granny Tulip.

At that moment, Appleby appeared in the doorway. The fifteen-year-old was very vivacious, with red hair and green eyes. She was the most volatile member of the family, a perennial teenager who never told the truth when a lie would do.

"What about Appleby?" she asked, sounding cross and suspicious.

"Appleby is Appleby," said Pilbeam. "She'll never be any different."

"I don't want to be," said Appleby. "Those bangs have gone right to your head!"

Pilbeam held her breath and did not laugh. Vinetta got up to go.

"Let's leave Granny in peace now. She has her work to do, and so have I."

After they were all gone, Tulip, following the careful directions Pilbeam had given her earlier, rang the booking office at His Majesty's Theatre Royal. She had felt a bit unsure at first of the wisdom of the venture, but Pilbeam was so certain and so determined that her grandmother had not argued.

"I'd like one seat in the stalls for *The Merchant of Venice* on Thursday, the twenty-seventh of January," said Tulip when her call was answered.

"One moment, please," said the girl on the other end of the line. Voices could be heard talking to each other in the office. Then the girl returned to the telephone and began, "We have . . ."

"It must be on a side aisle, near an exit," Tulip interrupted.

"No problem," said the girl. "Seat 33N is exactly what you require. We'll post the ticket out to you, if you would like to give me particulars of your credit card . . ."

So it was all arranged. Pilbeam, a week come Thursday, was to have her first ever visit to the theater. A real, happening-now thing, not a fictional memory.

❧ 2 ❧

Dear Bunty

In the upstairs sitting-room at Number 9 Brocklehurst Grove, Anthea Fryer sat in the armchair by the bay window. It was two months since her campaign to save Brocklehurst Grove had ended with a triumphant appearance on the roof. It had been exhilarating to be up there with the television cameras trained on her, zoom lenses giving a close-up of her smiling face as she fixed one end of the victory banner to the chimney pot ... And now, having risen to so great a height, she had descended to the depths. Flu, foul weather, and a letter from her brother had reduced her to a state of total misery. She bit her lip as she read his words again.

Dear Bunty,

What on earth possessed you to make such an exhibition of yourself? We saw it on TV even down here in Cornwall. It was one of those programs about the people versus the planners. When you came on we couldn't believe our eyes.

It was all very worthy, I know, and I'm glad you succeeded, but don't you think that climb onto the roof was taking it a bit too far? You'd already won by then. I bet Dad put you up to it.

Enough said.

What is happening at the gallery? I tried ringing you there but the line was dead. Bills not paid? I still think you should pack it all in and go to college. It's not too late. There are plenty of mature students these days. Don't let Dad talk you into any more mad schemes. I honestly wouldn't trust him with little Gemma's money box. He's well-meaning, but he hasn't a clue.

And what's this about Mother doing a concert tour in Lanarkshire whilst Dad goes house-hunting in Hong Kong? Or is it the other way round? Garbled version from Michael after Dad rang here from a payphone in the wilds somewhere. I tried ringing the studio, but a young woman there said something about Perth. When I asked whether she meant in Scotland or in Australia, she took offense for some reason and rang off.

So how about giving us a ring or, better still, send us one of your nice long letters. We all love to hear from you. Linda and the kids send their love. Take care, sis, and don't do anything else daft. Trying to outdo Father is really a dead loss. You're worth ten of him, if you would only wake up to the fact.

Love,
Tristram

Anthea put the letter down. It should have made her feel angry, but she was at too low an ebb to make such a spirited response. She sighed and turned her attention half-heartedly to the street below. There were no net curtains at Number 9, so her view was totally unimpeded.

A dark green Bentley came out of the drive at Number 3 on the other side of the square. In the dull quiet of the early afternoon even that was an event. Then Anthea looked across at Number 5. Activity there. A girl in a red winter coat coming out of the gate with another, possibly younger, girl, dressed in a pale blue anorak and jeans.

Anthea began to wonder, in an aimless way, about the family who lived there. Those girls didn't look odd. They looked no different from any other girls. But that chap Arnold or Albert something, who represented them when everyone in the street was trying to save their homes from being demolished, had warned her against troubling the family at Number 5. He had said that they were all reclusive and excessively nervous of speaking to outsiders.

I'll become a recluse, thought Anthea, wincing as she thought of Tristram's letter. I'll never go out again. Tristram was right. I did make a fool of myself. It makes me burn to think of it now. And Tris was right about the money, too. The gallery had failed and all the money Granma had left her was lost. The gallery had been Dad's idea of a good investment.

Now he was prowling round Scotland, house-hunting and filming some saga for the small screen. And Mother was in Hong Kong with the London Sinfonia.

And here was their only daughter, stuck in Brocklehurst Grove, with no immediate aim in life, nursing a cold and feeling extremely sorry for herself. She felt drained of energy. She had minded terribly the failure of the gallery and the way Stephen had simply faded from her life in the midst of all her troubles. Why had he bothered to get to know her? Why had he ever pretended to care for her in the first place? No wonder her mother had called him "the wavering wimp." On a better day, Anthea would have been healthily angry with her ex-boyfriend. But today, all she could feel was that everything in her life was doomed to failure.

Even the weather was not cheering. Outside it was cold and bleak, though dry at last after days of rain. From the gateway of Number 5, a frumpish lady wheeled out a large green perambulator.

Another recluse, thought Anthea. Arnold, Albert, or whatever his name was, must surely have been exaggerating. There was more coming and going at Number 5 than at any other house in the street—though that wouldn't have been difficult.

Connie Witherton came into the room, breaking in on these thoughts. She was the only other person living in the house at that time. For twenty years, in various places, she had been a sort of housekeeper for the Fryers. By now they all regarded her as a member of the family. A blunt-spoken Yorkshirewoman, she could honestly claim to have been almost a mother to Anthea, and whenever she did so, Loretta, Anthea's real mother, would simply smile vaguely and agree.

Anthea looked up when she heard Connie come in.

"Tristram's been nagging at me again," she said, handing Connie the letter. "But he's right this time. That's the worst of it."

"I don't think he's fair on you, Anthea," said Connie

after she had read it. "What right has he to criticize what you do? He's away in Cornwall with his wife and kids. We don't hear from him from one month's end to the next. What you do is none of his business."

Anthea still looked miserable.

"But he is right, Connie," she said. "I do some stupid things, and I never seem to learn. I'm always jumping in with both feet."

Connie looked at her more closely. Anthea's eyes were red-rimmed and her mouth was set in misery. People who had seen the smiling blonde on the rooftop did not know the half of it. She had looked and sounded so confident. That was her face for the world outside. But any member of her family, including Connie, could say a word or raise an eyebrow and knock her confidence to smithereens. Since Stephen had left and the gallery had closed, she felt more vulnerable than ever.

"Come on," said Connie, "tea's ready. You're coming downstairs with me and we'll have a nice meal and a long chat. You're on your own far too much these days. You should get yourself out and about more."

"I'm going out on Thursday," said Anthea defensively. "I'm going to the theater with Bobby Barras. A belated celebration for saving the Grove."

"Him at Number 1?"

"Yes," said Anthea.

"He's too old for you. A widower with a teenage son. He must be at least forty."

Anthea laughed self-consciously. "Not quite," she said. "Besides, we're just having a civilized night out. I'm not going to marry him!"

"That's better," said Connie. "Keep laughing. Now let's go down for some tea."

The unsuspecting residents of Number 5 Brocklehurst Grove were going about their lives that day without the least idea that anyone was observing their movements.

Pilbeam and Appleby decided to go shopping.

"I need a new pair of dark glasses," said Pilbeam. "Some that I can wear indoors without looking too odd. A pair with black rims and smoky glass should do it. You can pop into Mr. Sutton's and see what he's got. Failing that, we'll go to Boots and you can help me choose a pair."

The strong, loving friendship that had grown between the two sisters had been strained since Pilbeam had acquired a new hairstyle and added two important years to her age.

"I don't like you being grown up," said Appleby. "It's a rotten idea. There'll be no more fun. You'll be too old. You'll start telling me what to do, like all the others."

"I'm not *that* much older," Pilbeam protested. "I *am* grown up, as grown up as I'll ever be. It honestly won't make very much difference."

But Pilbeam had already started to do all sorts of irritating things. She helped Vinetta with the household chores, making a very constructive contribution to tidying the cupboards. She typed manuscripts for Sir Magnus and gave him a genuine filing system based upon the alphabet, of all things. And, worst of all, she began to wear skirts instead of jeans. Vinetta had just bought her a very stylish red coat with a fur-lined hood and a belt round the waist.

15

It was intended for her visit to the theater, but Pilbeam wanted to try it before then.

"I'll wear my new coat today," she said. "Then it won't feel strange when I wear it for the theater."

Appleby grimaced.

"I don't know what you want to go *there* for," she said. "It'll be dead boring. Shakespeare might as well be on another planet as far as I care. I'd have come with you if it had been a pop concert. But Shakespeare! I wouldn't go if you begged me to."

"I'm not asking you to go," said Pilbeam. "I don't even want you to go. I don't mean that in any nasty way. I just know that if you were sitting there not enjoying yourself and looking bored it would spoil it for me, too. Next time there's a pop concert, we'll go together. We can both enjoy that."

The words were kindly meant, the tone was friendly, but it was too much for Appleby.

"Don't you talk down to me, Pilbeam," she fumed. "I don't need you to go anywhere with me. I was sneaking off to the pictures and even to the odd disco before ever you . . ."

Her voice froze as she realized what she had been about to say. There was a shocked silence. It was such a cruel way to refer to Pilbeam's long, lifeless years in a trunk in the attic. That period of Pilbeam's life was known to exist, but was seldom mentioned. Other memories had been superimposed and had almost, but not quite, wiped it out.

Pilbeam tied the belt on her new coat and looked at herself in the hall mirror. She was deeply hurt and trying not to show it.

"Ready?" she said to Appleby.

"Yes," said her sister in a voice so subdued it was barely audible.

It was an uneasy outing. Pilbeam felt self-conscious in her new coat. Appleby felt shabby in her old anorak. But the feeling went beyond the clothes they wore. These were just an outward symbol of an inner truth.

"Things *are* different, Pilbeam," said Appleby as they trudged back home late in the afternoon, their umbrellas held up against the rain that had begun to fall. "I don't care what you say. Things will never be the same again."

Pilbeam gave her a look of sympathy.

"You may be right," she said. "But that doesn't mean that things have to be worse. I can't help being grown up. It just happened."

❦ 3 ❦

Going to the Theater

Joshua's route to work was along three miles of back streets behind the main road. He would hurry there each evening with his head deep in his coat collar, or even covered by a hood, looking directly at no one but always aware of everybody and everything within sight or sound. He was quick, quiet and cautious as a soldier on enemy terrain.

"You will have to take Pilbeam to the theater," said Vinetta. "It is on your way to work, and even the timing will be just about right."

They were in the kitchen, late afternoon, pretending to drink tea. Joshua looked up over the rim of his cup, but said nothing. Vinetta recognized that look.

"Somebody has to take her," she said. "I can't have her going out as late as that on her own."

"She says she's eighteen now," said Joshua, looking truculent. "She's used to going out on her own. She won't want to go along the back streets with me, and there's no way I am going to go along the main road. I know where I feel safe and I know where I don't."

"What Pilbeam wants or doesn't want has nothing to do with it," said Vinetta, smiling but firm. "What you will or won't do has nothing to do with it. She is not going alone. You are taking her, Josh. I have made up my mind."

"And who will be bringing her back?" asked Joshua. "It'll be much later then. And I won't be available as an escort. I'll be at work."

"I have considered that," said Vinetta. "Soobie goes jogging at all hours. He can jog up the High Street in time to meet Pilbeam as she comes out."

Joshua was about to say something else, but he decided not to. There was no point in arguing with Vinetta when her mind was made up. He would have much preferred Pilbeam not to go to the theater at all. He thought it a very risky undertaking. To have sounded other than surly about taking her there might have been taken to mean that he approved!

Sir Magnus was more outspoken in *his* disapproval.

"Of all the tomfoolery," he said to Tulip when she told him of it. "What does she want to go gadding there for? Have we not had enough trouble? Is she on the look-out for another young man? We've never had this bother with Appleby."

Tulip looked very severe.

"That is unfair, Magnus," she said. "Pilbeam was very fond of Albert. They had got to know one another. When he had to go, she felt it very deeply, but she accepted the inevitable. There is no way she would go out looking for more trouble. Our grandchildren have a right to some freedom. You know Pilbeam well enough. She will be very cautious."

"She may be cautious," said Magnus, "and she might not go looking for trouble, but trouble can find her all the same."

He leaned forward in his bed so that his purple foot, escaping the counterpane, touched the floor. His black beady eyes were his youngest feature, giving the impression of a vigorous mind. His white walrus moustache and bushy eyebrows made him look, if anything, older than the seventy years to which he laid claim.

The occasions when Sir Magnus left his bed were very rare and special. Last year's enforced trip to the country had been traumatic. The intrusion of Albert Pond, a flesh-and-blood human being, into their life had been terrible to *him,* whatever the rest of the family might think. Sir Magnus was a scholar. Editors of the journals to which he contributed learned articles never knew that the writer was other than a very distinguished man. In the past forty years the pretend had grown and developed. It is quite probable that Sir Magnus Mennym M.A. (Oxon) knew at least as much as anybody in the English-speaking world about Roundheads and Cavaliers. The pretend degree, conferred upon him by Kate, was well-supported by genuine scholarship. Yet the events of the past few years had left their mark. Time, he had begun to realize, could not really stand still forever. He feared what might come next with a dread that was becoming paranoid.

Tulip knew him. She hoped that gradually, one step at a time, she might be able to restore her husband to a less anxious frame of mind. Pilbeam's visit to the theater might even help. Look, Magnus, Tulip could say, Pilbeam went to the theater, and the sky didn't fall in.

So when Thursday evening came, Tulip insisted upon Pilbeam going to Granpa's room to show off her outfit before she left for the theater. She had warned Magnus to be gracious, throwing him the pearl of wisdom that what could not be cured must be endured. Vinetta came too, prepared to defend her daughter if necessary.

Pilbeam stood in the middle of the room, knowing she looked her best, and feeling quite pleased with herself. She had replaced the tie belt on the red coat with a broad, black one in tooled leather with a buckle. She was wearing the spectacles Appleby had chosen from Mr. Sutton's shop—large, thin black frames surrounding smoky plain glass lenses. They were not cheap rejects by any means, but Tulip had paid for them ungrudgingly. Pilbeam's ensemble was completed with a pair of black kid gloves and knee-length fashion boots that matched the belt. There was an aura about her that would have drawn glances in any crowd.

"You look wonderful," said Granpa. "I'm proud of you." Then he reached under his pillow for his money pouch and gave Pilbeam a note.

"For your program," he said, "and taxi fares."

No one in the family had ever traveled in any form of public transport. It was considered much too intimate, much too dangerous.

"I couldn't use a taxi, Granpa," said Pilbeam. "I shall just have to walk. It's not so very far, you know."

"A taxi would be safer than walking. I don't approve of your walking at this time of day. And it is not the same as traveling in a bus or a train. You would sit alone in the back. The driver would be in front. It will be dark. The risk is minimal."

Vinetta thought of the minimal risk and said, "I prefer no risk at all."

She told him of the arrangements she had made for Pilbeam to be escorted there and back.

"You are right, I suppose," said Granpa pensively, even more conscious of risk than Vinetta would ever be. "Yes. You *are* right. Better safe than sorry."

He turned to Pilbeam and said, "You are quite sure about going there? You have considered the dangers?"

"Yes," said Pilbeam, giving Granpa a look that warned him to say no more.

She tried to give him back his money, now that it had been decided that she would not be taking a taxi.

"Keep it," said Granpa. "Do what you like with it. But I would like to see the program. I used to enjoy the

21

theater in my young days. It will bring back happy memories.''

They all knew how much and how little that meant. The words had cost Sir Magnus some effort. Deep down, he was so disapproving of this outing that he would have loved to forbid it. Having accepted that it would take place, he needed to insulate it, to wrap it round with protective pretends.

When they went downstairs again, Joshua was already standing in the hall, becoming impatient.

''Time we were away,'' he said. ''Got your ticket?''

''Yes,'' said Pilbeam.

Father and daughter set off briskly into the darkness. Once they had left the Grove behind them, Joshua turned down the first side street onto a route that would add at least ten minutes to their journey, but this was his usual way to work and he had no intention of changing it.

Pilbeam was not at all comfortable going down badly-lit back streets and tripping along quickly to keep pace with her father. She kept worrying in case her little heels caught in uneven pavements. It was as if she were a child again, a five-year-old trotting along beside her parents. Embedded memory, silly embedded memory! She did not feel in the least bit elegant now! What is more, she was anxious in case they should miss the turn-off for the theater. But when they came at last to Kyd Street, Joshua stopped abruptly and looked along the unlit, narrow alley.

''It's along there,'' he said.

At the other end of the alley they could see signs of a broad, well-lit street.

"I'll take you to the far corner," said Joshua. "Then I'll have to put on some speed or I'll be late for work."

"No need," said Pilbeam. "I'll just leave you here. I can go the rest of the way by myself."

"Along *there!*" said Joshua, looking at the murky street that was no better than a back lane. "No you'll not. Your mother would be furious if I let you go along there by yourself. Come on. Walk a bit faster."

Together they went along the lane, walking quickly on rough cobblestones, past the rear wall of a restaurant, then the closed double doors of a side entrance to the theater. When they came to the corner, there was suddenly a blaze of light and life. Streetlamps were augmented by lamps on wrought-iron stands attached to the pillars of the theater's huge portico. Groups of people were going inside. It was all lively bustle.

"You'll be all right now. Don't speak to anybody, and be sure to wait for Soobie when you come out," said Joshua as he melted back into the darkness of the alley and sped on his way to work. Like his father, he was worried about Pilbeam's venture into public life. His brusqueness was his way of showing it, the only way he knew.

Pilbeam, so brave in preparing to go, so determined to have this extra dimension to her life, looked at the crowd, and felt nervous and foolish and out of place. As in a dream, she walked into the foyer, across the carpeted floor, past the gaudy kiosk, and through the doors that led to the stalls. A girl in an overall, standing in a corner of the softly-lit lobby, took her ticket, tore it in two, threaded one end onto a string and handed Pilbeam the stub.

"Left-hand side," the girl said without looking at Pilbeam.

"Thank you," said Pilbeam, and hurried down the ramp and into the auditorium. She bought a program and slipped into her seat. The worst was over. She could hide behind the program till the lights went down.

Bobby Barras and Anthea Fryer had seats in the Dress Circle. They came into the foyer just behind Pilbeam. Anthea tugged Bobby's sleeve.

"I'm sure that's our neighbor," she said.

"Who?" said Bobby.

"That girl over there—the one in the red coat. I saw her the other day coming out of the gate of Number 5."

"She doesn't look like a recluse to me," said Bobby. "You must be mistaken." He had heard all about the mysterious residents of Number 5 who were on no account to be disturbed. At the time when they were all trying to save the Grove, Albert Pond had told Anthea a very convincing tale about his "cousins" who had a paranoid fear of the outside world. It was, after all, very nearly true. That their fear was down to something quite other than collective neurosis was a situation no one could ever have imagined.

"I am beginning to think that relative of theirs, goodness knows why, was just spinning us a yarn," said Anthea. "I have been watching Number 5. They come and go like anybody else. And I am quite sure it is her. That long, black hair, and the way she walks and holds herself, are very distinctive. Just to look at her makes me feel a frump."

Anthea put on no airs for Bobby. To him, this frankness was one of her most endearing qualities. He had become a good friend and she felt she could talk to him as freely as to one of her own family. It was a pleasant change. On this personal level she was often awkward with strangers, worrying too much about what they would think of her. It was easier to talk to a crowd than to be comfortable chatting with one person. And her assertiveness toward the outside world was probably a side-effect of her failure ever to rebel against her parents, or even Connie. The public and the private Anthea were two different people.

Pilbeam disappeared into the Stalls. Her neighbors from Brocklehurst Grove went up the curving staircase to the Circle. They settled into seats near the front. Anthea began to inspect the audience with her opera glasses.

"She's there," she said. "I'm sure it's her. She's sitting on the end of the row, near the center exit. Look."

Bobby wasn't interested but he grinned at Anthea, took a brief look through the glasses, and handed them back.

The lights dimmed, the curtains parted, and the play began.

4

A Close Encounter

Pilbeam was entranced by everything—from the lighting on the stage to the warmth of the listening audience who stopped being polite and pompous (pretending to read the Bard from morning till night and to have seen all the best performances at Stratford) and became genuinely engrossed in the play. Appleby should have been there after all. Even Appleby would have been enthralled by it.

Pilbeam sorrowed for Shylock. That poor man! Spat upon and spurned, robbed and betrayed by his own daughter, driven to such madness that he almost takes another man's life . . . The outsider recognized the outsider. When Jessica ran away from her father, Pilbeam thought of Vinetta, worrying herself sick over Appleby's escapades. And what if Shylock *did* sound more interested in his missing jewels and money . . . was that not just like Sir Magnus, hiding one feeling under another less painful? Anger is good at masking grief.

In the interval, Pilbeam had courage to lay aside her program. The man sitting next to her was being attentive to his talkative wife. Pilbeam looked round the hall. She gasped as she saw, four or five rows in front and away to her right, a profile she recognized, a young man talking to a girl with long, dark hair. In a provincial city, with only one large theater and the Royal Shakespeare Company on a brief annual visit, it was not such an improbable coincidence. This was indeed Pilbeam's final sight of Albert Pond, that love of hers she had never thought to see again. He had a girlfriend. Pilbeam, loving him still, was glad.

The first thing Pilbeam did as the final curtain fell was to pull her fur-lined hood well over her head. An unnecessary precaution, but never had Pilbeam been part of such a crowd in a space so enclosed. She walked quickly out of the auditorium. Then up the ramp she went, through the outer doors and into the street, though still under the theater's well-lit portico. She looked along toward the corner that led to Kyd Street, expecting to see Soobie standing in the shadows. He was not there.

Bobby and Anthea came out of the theater and began walking down toward the spot where they had parked the car.

"There she is," said Anthea, spotting the distinctive figure in the red coat. "She must be trying to get a taxi."

Pilbeam was looking round uncomfortably, unsure whether to set off walking home alone. But Soobie might come along Kyd Street, or he might be jogging up the High Street. They could miss each other. If Soobie arrived and she was not there, he would be anxious. In such circumstances, Appleby would have strode off regardless, and would have thought it served Soobie right for being late. Pilbeam was much too considerate even to think that way.

*　　*　　*

"Let's offer her a lift," said Anthea. "She can only say no. There's no harm in asking."

Before Bobby could stop her, she was striding across the pavement toward the girl in the red coat.

Pilbeam was looking toward the alley, still wondering what to do. She had no idea that anyone had noticed her, but when she heard a voice behind her say, "We're going your way. Can we give you a lift?" she knew in a flash that this must be one of their neighbors. The danger was dire. What on earth was she to do?

At that moment, Soobie jogged out of the dark alley and took in the situation at a glance.

The blonde woman with her hand out about to tap his sister on the shoulder was surely their neighbor, the one who had been so busy about saving the Grove. Soobie spurted forward, head down like a rugby player, grabbed Pilbeam by the arm and steered her into the darkness of the alleyway.

"Jog!" he said. "Jog for all you're worth!"

They ran along the narrow, cobbled street and out of sight.

Anthea, left standing, couldn't believe it. How could anyone, recluse or no recluse, have such appalling bad manners?

"Maybe she didn't hear you," said Bobby when he reached her side.

"She heard all right," said Anthea. "That must have been her brother who pulled her away. I thought I recognized the tracksuit. He's another weirdo. I've seen him jogging at midnight, but never during the day."

"Talk about nosy neighbors!" said Bobby with a laugh as they got into the car.

"Interested in my fellow men," said Anthea a bit frostily. "Just interested."

They did not drive home in silence. Anthea was incapable of being frosty for long. The evening ended as it had begun, in friendship. And when Bobby suggested another outing, Anthea did not refuse.

"Do you think we could slow down now?" said Pilbeam as they turned the corner out of Kyd Street. "I trotted all the way here. I don't want to jog all the way home. It does nothing for my image!"

Soobie slowed to a walk.

"Did you enjoy the play?" he said.

"It was wonderful," said Pilbeam. "We have too few happening-now things in our lives. But I think I might be scared to risk going again."

"Because of the neighbors?" said Soobie. "I see your point. That was that Fryer woman. She strikes me as being a busybody. She could be dangerous."

Pilbeam agreed. She never mentioned seeing Albert.

❦ 5 ❦

A Family Conference

"**W**e must not court disaster," said Sir Magnus, looking round solemnly at the assembled family. Everyone was there except Googles. It was their first meeting in Granpa's room for many months. Sir Magnus had called the conference on the Saturday after Pilbeam's outing to the theater. She had told him all about the play, had given him the program, and had explained why she could never go again. Anthea Fryer. The masterful blonde who lived at Number 9.

Granpa had taken it much more seriously than Pilbeam expected. It became a momentous event that needed to be dealt with as family business. He called a meeting for Saturday so that Joshua could be present. And at seven p.m., when they were all gathered round his bed, Sir Magnus plunged straight into a long explanation of how great was this new, though insidious, threat to the family. He was seated bolt upright, unsupported by his many pillows, leaning forward so that his purple foot, which always hung over the side of the bed, was actually touching the floor.

"This Fryer woman," he said, "is as great a danger as the planners who wanted to destroy the street, possibly even greater. Planners are not interested in people. This young woman is.''

"I think you are exaggerating, Magnus," said Tulip, trying to calm all their fears. "We will ignore her, as we have always done. She has lived in the street for about five years, I should think.''

"Four years and seven months," said Soobie, who was always very precise about the dates when people moved in and out of the neighborhood. From his seat in the lounge window he had a ringside view of every disgorging pantechnicon. The Fryers were remarkable because a second special van had delivered a grand piano.

Tulip gave Soobie an impatient look before continuing.

"This woman," she said, "may move away at any time. She and her family will probably be as transient as others have been. Her prime concern in saving the Grove was probably to ensure that her house should not become unsalable. I don't blame her for that, but, take it from me, that will be the truth of it.''

Magnus was scornful.

"We are talking about here and now," he said. "Next week, not some hypothetical next year. There is every chance that Miss Fryer will speak to Pilbeam the very next time she leaves the house. Then what? And she may know by sight any one of us that is in the habit of going out into the street, for whatever reason. She is dangerous.''

Miss Quigley looked smug.

"She would not know *me,*" she said, "not even by sight from a distance. I have a talent for fading into the background and being totally inconspicuous. It has to do with being nondescript, I suppose.''

There was always a bite in Miss Quigley's blandly delivered statements. Soobie alone recognized and appreciated the dryness of her wit.

"That could be useful," said Sir Magnus, looking directly at the nanny for the first time in ages. "It is certainly worth considering. We may need you. We will need you!"

The others looked puzzled.

"As I see it," continued Sir Magnus, speaking now to everybody, "we must all stay indoors for a month or two, till Miss Fryer loses any interest she might have in the residents of Number 5."

"Stay indoors!" said Appleby. "For a *month* or two? You must be joking! Easy enough for you, Granpa. You haven't been out of that bed since Christmas. And then it was a major event. I'm not staying cooped up in the house for days on end. I go places. I see things. I buy things. That's what life's about."

Vigorous as usual, blunt and determined, but no match for her grandfather on this occasion. His black button eyes glared at her.

"You will do what you are told, young lady, or you might find yourself shut up in the airing cupboard. *That* is really being cooped up. Remember?"

Appleby seethed, but said no more.

"I suppose I could get by without going out," said Tulip, "but it will be inconvenient never to go to the wool shop. I have my work to do, you know, Magnus. I will need the wool."

The only place Tulip ever went to was, in fact, the wool shop. Infrequently and with a sense of occasion, she took off her checked pinafore and dressed up to go out. She would wear her one and only outdoor coat, dark gray, in a princess style with a silver fur collar and a half-belt on the back. On her head she would wear a matching felt hat with a veil that she pulled down over her brow. The clothes were old-fashioned, but they served their purpose. The woman inside them was totally unrecognizable, but obviously a lady.

"What about the Post Office?" said Appleby as her mind leapt from Granny's wool to Granpa's manuscripts. "I always take your mail to the Post Office. That's a necessity."

"And what about the Market?" said Vinetta. "There are always things we need at the Market—light bulbs, thread, all manner of things. It would be impossible for me to stay at home for weeks at a time."

"And I," said Miss Quigley, "have to take Googles to the park."

Magnus let them talk. He looked expectantly at his son, who caught the glance and gave a dour reply.

"I go to work," he said, "and that is that. I go in the evening. I return early in the morning. No one ever so much as crosses my path."

"A fair point," conceded his father.

"I jog," said Soobie, "but only after dark."

It was a new pleasure for the blue Mennym and not one he would willingly give up.

With memories of his days in the Royal Navy, wartime days when battle strategy was so vital, Magnus considered the situation. Brocklehurst Grove occupied three sides of a square round a green in the center of which stood the statue of Matthew James Brocklehurst. Looking across to the right from a first floor window, the Mennyms could see Number 1 at the end of the street, where lived Bobby Barras, fire chief, and friend of Anthea Fryer. Looking across to the left, at the other end of the street, was Number 9, home of the dreaded Anthea. There was no back entrance to Number 5. Where their garden ended, over a high, woody hedge and a stout fence, another long garden began, a neglected tract of land belonging to a house in the old Georgian terrace that was waiting forlornly to be demolished.

"This is a tight situation," said Magnus, whose serious concern could not prevent him from enjoying the challenge. Here at last was the opportunity to protect his family from the outside world by taking positive steps, instead of just lying awake at night fearing the worst. *Now* they would have to listen to him.

"We could regard ourselves as being potentially under siege," he said. "There is no crisis yet, but we must be ready for anything."

The others said nothing and waited. Magnus sat back and clasped his hands across his chest, pressing his thumbs together in a manner that looked decisive. Then he spoke again in slow Churchillian tones.

"Joshua will—for the present—go to his place of employment as usual. His hours are his best protection, especially at this time of year."

Joshua looked relieved and lost all interest in anything else that might be said. He had the sort of mind that took short cuts to reality. He was in total agreement with his father over the need for the other Mennyms to stay at home. And he was absolutely confident that no outsider would ever find *him* out.

"Same applies to my jogging," said Soobie.

"A non-essential activity," said his grandfather, "but I suppose you're right."

"What about the shopping?" asked Vinetta.

"That," said her father-in-law, "is where we come to our secret weapon. All of the shopping, all of the visits to the Post Office or the cash machine, must be done by Miss Quigley. She will also go to the wool shop for Tulip. She is right. Her ability to go unnoticed is unsurpassed."

Miss Quigley was flattered to be so publicly recognized as the one who was unnoticeable, but she was astute enough to know that there had to be a catch somewhere.

"The old green perambulator," said Sir Magnus, "is quite another matter. It is conspicuous. Babies are conspicuous. They are an excuse for people to speak, to look and to admire. In normal circumstances, Miss Quigley's own appearance would be enough to deflect attention. But these are not normal circumstances. A woman over there" (he flung his arm out in the general direction of Number 9) "is watching us. She may be waiting her chance to pounce. Googles and the perambulator must not leave this house again until we are sure that all is safe."

"No park?" said Miss Quigley. "Googles loves the park, even in winter. She likes to watch me feed the ducks."

Sir Magnus gave her a look of disdain.

"Wimpey tells me we have robins in the back garden," he said. "Feed them, if that is what takes your fancy."

Miss Quigley was uneasy, but she accepted her new

role as forager in enemy territory. She visualized it as being a small addition to her duties as nanny, and not one that would encroach too much upon her time for painting. Appleby still looked disgruntled. Pilbeam, thinking over all that had been said, was suddenly ashamed of herself.

"This is all my fault," she said. "We would have been much safer if I hadn't gone to the theater. Wearing a red coat too, and trying to look so smart. So much for being grown up and seeking new experiences!"

"Don't blame yourself," said Vinetta. "Any one of us could have been observed at any time. And," she lowered her voice and looked cautiously toward the old man, "I do think your grandfather might be over-reacting."

❧ 6 ❧

Miss Quigley On Call

Two or three times a year a delivery van brought a parcel of flat-packs to 5 Brocklehurst Grove. Poopie and Wimpey were always delighted when this happened. The parcel was for their grandmother and consisted of a pile of shaped and printed cardboard sheets that needed to be folded correctly to turn them into boxes. The outside of each box was deep green with the name *tulipmennym* scrawled all over at different angles most artistically. In these boxes, Tulip used to pack the sweaters and cardigans she made for Harrods to sell. This had been her business for many years. She had designed the boxes before ever approaching the London store, knowing instinctively that packaging was important.

Poopie and Wimpey, over the years, had become expert at assembling the flat-packs. They knew exactly how the folds went and where the tabs fitted. And they *loved* doing it!

"You two are really very good at that," Granny Tulip would say. "I'd get into a right tangle if I had to do it myself."

The problem came when half a dozen boxes were ready packed, with tissue paper covering the soft newness of the wool. Who was to take them to the Post Office?

It had always been Appleby's job, but under the new regime there was only one errand-girl. And she was well over fifty and considerably over-worked.

"Hortensia," said Tulip in her pleasantest voice, "I know it's an imposition, but would you be so kind as to take some packages to the Post Office for me? They need to go Guaranteed Delivery, or whatever it is they call it now."

Miss Quigley gave Tulip an icy look. Diffident people and super-confident people are always poles apart, no matter what the situation. This particular situation was not of the best to start with. For the past three weeks, Hortensia had shopped for Vinetta, posted things for Sir Magnus, bought newspapers and magazines and generally fetched and carried for every member of the family till she felt like the most menial of servants. They had even begun to ask her to take things up and downstairs for them. Her role as nanny was neglected. Poor little Googles lay in the nursery unfed, unchanged and unburped, like a doll some child no longer wants. She slept most of the time. Awake, her flecked hazel eyes looked listlessly at the ceiling. She did not even bother to rattle her favorite pink plastic bear. It was worse than the years before she had a nanny. Vinetta, always in demand with the rest of the family, always able to find something useful to do, would forget all about Googles till bedtime, then pop in to carry her baby to the night nursery. A brief hug. A guilty sigh. And that was that.

"How many of these do you expect me to take at a time?" asked Miss Quigley, looking doubtfully at the boxes. Had Tulip been at all sensitive she might have detected the hostility in Miss Quigley's voice.

"Four will do," she answered calmly, with no regard at all for the bulkiness of the packages. "They are not really heavy."

"They are bulky," said Miss Quigley through lips that hardly opened.

Appleby had usually taken six at a time, packing them into a very large sports bag. It was electric blue, imitation leather, with *Adidas* written in huge white letters on the sides. When this was shown to Miss Quigley, she gave it a look of contempt.

"That," she said, "is too conspicuous for me to use. If you think a green pram would attract unwelcome attention, you have to realize how much attention that object would merit, especially carried by a woman of my age and dignity."

The last word was said with a mocking half-smile. Hortensia Quigley's muted sarcasm was individual to her. The Mennyms, for all their varied talents, never quite understood it.

Without answering, Tulip went to the cupboard in the corner of the breakfast room and dragged out an old tartan shopping trolley hooked onto a rather lopsided frame.

"That should do," she said. "No one will ever notice that."

"It's very, very shabby," Hortensia said, feeling embarrassed but goaded into a protest. She had no personal vanity and no pretensions, but she loathed shabbiness. Her self-respect was being eroded. The dirty old trolley was just another straw on a camel's back about ready to break.

Tulip was a good bit shorter than Miss Quigley, but she had a way of drawing herself up to her full height that would have made her seem the tallest person in any room. In a quiet but imperious voice she said, "It's the best I can do. I hope you won't have to be troubled much longer. We are just waiting for Sir Magnus to give the all-clear. When he feels it is safe again, we'll all be able to go back to normal. This will probably be the only delivery I shall have to ask you to make."

So, reluctantly, Hortensia took the trolley full of boxes to the Post Office. Her shoes were polished, her coat well-brushed, and all her clothing was fresh and clean. It did not make her conspicuous, but it dissociated her from the despicable trolley with its torn flap fitting badly over the four boxes. People are what people wear!

The man behind the Post Office counter, middle-aged, gray-haired and preoccupied, accepted the parcels, filled out the receipts and handed them over without a word or a look. Miss Quigley bought two books of postage stamps for Sir Magnus. If there was to be a siege, he had argued, it was wise to lay in supplies. A few at a time. A squirrel's hoard of stamps and stationery.

❦ 7 ❦

Sounds Easy

Tony Barras at sixteen was taller and slimmer than his father, but he had the same black hair and deep blue eyes. Father and son had lived at Number 1 Brocklehurst Grove with Great Aunts Jane and Eliza for the past three years. In term time, Tony was away at school in Harrogate. So he never really got to know the neighbors, even by sight. Maybe it was because the girls at Number 5 had always been young ladies and he had only just become a young man, but this year was the first time he had ever noticed them. It was the last week in March and he was home for Easter.

He was just closing the front gate, off for a morning in town, when he caught sight of two girls about his own age emerging from Number 5 and striding along the street in his direction. They looked bright and confident, not at all like the "weirdos" Anthea and Dad talked about. Instead of going straight out onto the High Street, Tony decided to take the long way round so he could pass the girls. He had quite made up his mind to say hello to them. Well, why not?

Then *they* saw *him*. As if they had suddenly collided with a force-field, they stopped abruptly, wheeled round and sped off in the opposite direction.

The whole of the Mennym household had by now continued in a state of self-imposed siege for nearly two months. At first it had not seemed too bad. The February weather had not been inviting, so no one envied Miss Quigley when she wrapped up warm to face the elements. She, poor lady, had been numbed as much by the tasks loaded upon her as by the chilling weather.

"Don't forget to take your umbrella," Tulip said each time she saw her to the door. But it was Vinetta who greeted her when she returned, and helped her with her packages, and made her sit by the fire in the lounge.

"Do have a biscuit," Vinetta would say warmly, after she had poured a pretend cup of tea for her friend and ally. Hortensia always managed to smile bravely, but there was really no going back to praising the little pink-iced biscuits and brushing imaginary crumbs from her lip. All that belonged to another era.

"I don't know how much more I can take," she said to Vinetta one day. "My job is looking after Googles. I hardly ever get to see her these days, and when I do she looks so limp and listless it breaks my heart. *You* must spend more time with her, Vinetta. Don't let the others monopolize you. And as for my painting, I haven't touched a brush since this all began."

She felt as if she had maybe said too much. She took a conciliatory sip from the china cup and nervously nibbled an ancient biscuit.

Vinetta looked concerned.

"It shouldn't last much longer," she said. "Nothing else has happened. No one has come near us. I'll have another word with Magnus. He must be made to see that he is being over-cautious."

Appleby was of the same opinion, though she expressed it somewhat differently as she fumed at Pilbeam in language that sounded more like Poopie in mid-tantrum. The sisters had been listening to records. Outside, the sun had put in one of his rare appearances.

"I want to go out," said Appleby. "This is just not good enough. Do you know what I think?"

Pilbeam was sitting on the floor, sorting through a pile of old records. She looked up at Appleby who was lying sprawled across the bed.

"Come on then," she said. "What great thought have you had this time?"

"I'm serious," said Appleby. "I think Granpa's flipped his lid. He's gone totally potty and we are all just letting him get away with it. Staying indoors, week after week, as if we were manning the barricades. He's stark raving bonkers, and they're all too scared of him to do anything about it."

Pilbeam looked doubtful. Privately, without going to such linguistic extremes, she almost shared Appleby's opinion. One visit to the theater . . . one word from a stranger . . . one tap on the shoulder . . . And suddenly all the world was their enemy.

"I wish now I hadn't told him about Anthea Fryer. After all, she only wanted to give me a lift. I wish now I'd had the presence of mind to say no thank you. One panic leads to another. I suppose we have to remember that being recognized is the biggest risk we can take. Granpa is only thinking of our good, our future."

Appleby looked unconvinced. Rebellion welled up inside her.

"I don't know why I am lying here grumbling," she said. "There is a solution. I'm getting ready and I'm going out!"

"They won't let you," said Pilbeam.

"They can't stop me," said Appleby, eyes flashing emerald green. "And I certainly won't be asking their permission."

Pilbeam faltered. She too was frustrated at being kept in, day after day. She too thought that Granpa was carrying caution to excess.

"I'll go with you," she said at last. "We'll be very careful and we won't stay out long. At least not the first time. It might even prove something. I know Mother would be pleased if we could go back to normal. And so would poor Miss Quigley."

Appleby looked enthusiastic. This was more like the old Pilbeam, in the days before she had become so tiresomely grown up.

"Jeans and anoraks," said Appleby. "Not that red coat."

They left the house very quietly, unobserved by anyone.

Miss Quigley was already out, away to the Market with a shopping list. Everyone else was busy. Soobie, seated in his chair by the window, might have seen them but he was absorbed in reading *Lord of the Rings* yet again.

They closed the gate behind them and set out toward the town end of the street, past Number 4, then Number 3. It was as they were passing the gate of Number 2 that they saw Tony Barras walking purposefully toward them. Pilbeam saw him first and immediately knew that he meant to speak to them. She grabbed Appleby's arm and wheeled her round to go the other way.

"That boy is going to speak to us," Pilbeam said. "Don't run, but hurry."

They soon put a few yards between themselves and danger.

"Is he following us?" asked Pilbeam, afraid to look round, but knowing that Appleby would be doing just that.

"No," said Appleby. "He's changed his mind. He's gone back, past Number 1."

With a wary look at Number 9, they left the Grove at the other end.

"We'll cross the main road straightaway, just in case. We can cross back later," said Pilbeam.

But the boy was out of sight and by now was on his way to town, well ahead of Appleby and Pilbeam.

"Let's go to *Sounds Easy,*" said Appleby. "It's ages since I bought a record."

Sounds Easy was one of Appleby's favorite shops. It sold new and second-hand records, everything from 78s to CDs. Appleby's taste did not include "the classics," but her knowledge of good popular music extended over

44

the past forty years and even longer. She had an enviable collection of Country and Western records.

From every point of view, *Sounds Easy* was a perfect shop for the Mennyms to use. It was not so very far from home—a goodish walk along main streets where it was easy for young people to be anonymous. To reach it, the girls had to go up the High Street past the Theater Royal to the junction with Albion Street, then along Albion Street as far as the Cathedral, behind which there was a mews enclosed by towering eighteenth century buildings, now used as offices with some of the ground floors converted into dark little shops. *Sounds Easy* was one of these shops, tucked away in a corner, a little below street level and approached down three well-worn steps. Inside, it extended far back as into a cave. The lighting was dim and barely adequate. Customers tended to bring their discs to the front windows, the better to read the labels. The proprietor had a counter placed strategically near the door. He was a man of indeterminate age with thinning sandy hair and an unkempt appearance, intensely interested in his stock, almost reluctant to sell it, and taciturn with his customers.

Appleby and Pilbeam went in and looked round. A scattering of other customers peered closely at possible purchases . . . Pilbeam headed for the CDs. Appleby was soon engrossed in Country and Western.

"Not a bad selection," said a voice beside her.

Appleby nearly dropped the precious 78 she was holding. A sidewise glance identified the speaker as the boy they'd seen in the Grove. Appleby should have known better, but the temptation to flirt with danger was too strong. After all, the shop was dimly lit and her tell-tale eyes were well-hidden. Her garish style of dress and make-up were surely disguise enough to make it possible to take a tiny risk.

"I have most of them," she said. "I've been collecting them for years." And Tony would never suspect how many years!

At the back of the shop, lit by a dull red light that revolved slowly, was an old juke box. Tony and Appleby drifted toward it and looked down at the list of records, all old. The box had been adapted to take twenty pence coins.

"What shall we have?" asked Tony, coin at the ready.

"Number 38," said Appleby.

Then the juke box came into action, swung a disc onto its geriatric turntable and began to play tinnily a sixties version of a thirties-type song . . .

Oh, lover, let my heart take wings
Don't tie it to your apron strings
I know that life would better be
If only you'd unfetter me . . .
Let me be . . . Set me free . . .

The send-up of Jessie Matthews was sung by a sweet-voiced young man with an impeccable English accent. Appleby joined in with the words, *sotto voce*. She had known them long enough.

"You know the words," said Tony.

"I know all the words to every song on that box," said Appleby.

"You don't!" said Tony, not in disbelief but in surprise and admiration.

"Yes I do," said Appleby. "In fact, last time I counted, I knew all the words of 529 songs."

"Wow!" said Tony. "Are you a good singer?"

Appleby giggled.

"Not so as you'd notice," she said, "but I honestly do know all the words."

"Do you sing in the bath?" said Tony. It was the obvious, bantering question.

But not for Appleby. She looked startled and suspicious, as if Tony had made some very improper suggestion. What a kinky idea! She had only once been in a bath full of water and that was horror of horrors and part of the worst experience of her life. And who in their right senses would want to sit and sing in an *empty* bath? That was a babyish, Googles pretend.

"No!" said Appleby sharply.

"Well, I do," said Tony, "and I bet my voice is much worse than yours. And I make up some of the words as I go along."

At that moment Pilbeam looked their way and was horrified. She put down the CD she'd been about to buy and walked swiftly toward her sister.

"Come on, Appleby," she said. "We're going to be late."

Then she marched her out of the shop before Tony could say another word.

The bell over the door jangled. The proprietor gave a careful glance to assure himself that these customers who had paid for nothing were leaving empty-handed.

Tony Barras stood beside the juke box. Appleby's departure had been so abrupt that he needed time to collect his wits.

Once outside the shop, Appleby and Pilbeam never looked back or slowed down till they reached the bottom of the High Street and were nearly home.

"You had no business to speak to that boy," said Pilbeam. "After all we said about being careful!"

"There was no harm done," said Appleby.

"No harm!" said Pilbeam. "He knows who you are and where you live. That might be harm enough."

"All right," said Appleby. "I won't do it again. But I do get away with it, you know. I'm different from the rest of you."

"Not that different," said Pilbeam.

They turned into Brocklehurst Grove.

"We'll not tell *them*," said Appleby. "If we do, we'll never hear the last of it. It was bad enough before."

Pilbeam agreed, but there was one point on which she took a firm stand.

"We won't be able to go out again," she said. "Not for a very long time. Granpa is right. It's too risky."

Soobie spotted them returning, but he said nothing.

❧ 8 ❧

A Clandestine Courtship

A few days after the visit to *Sounds Easy,* Appleby
looked out of the lounge window and was startled to see
Tony Barras walking up the front path. No one else was
in the lounge at the time. Soobie was listening to the radio
in his own room. Appleby rushed out to the hall and
waited for the bell to ring. What she would have done if
it had rung is far from clear. Even she might have hesitated
before opening the door.

Fortunately, there was no ring at the doorbell. Instead,
to Appleby's intense delight, a note fell through the letter-
box onto the doormat. She picked it up, and as expected,
saw that it was addressed to "Appleby," just the one
name, the strange name Tony had heard and remembered
from the record shop.

"What's that just come in the door?" called Tulip from
the breakfast-room.

"Nothing, Gran," said Appleby. "Just an advert for
double-glazing."

She hurried to her room and sat down on the floor with
her back to the door. Until she had read the letter she did
not want to risk Pilbeam walking in on her. That was

the worst of Pilbeam, thought Appleby as she opened the envelope, she would just walk in without even knocking. And she was so fussy about everything, especially now she was eighteen.

Dear Appleby, the letter began, *It was great fun talking to you the other day. I wish your sister (it was your sister, wasn't it?) hadn't made you leave so suddenly. My dad says not to trouble your family because you don't like to mix with us, so I am taking a bit of a risk writing to you. I only hope you are allowed to read a note addressed to you, and that I won't land you in trouble by writing. If you can manage to write back, perhaps we could arrange to meet some time and go out somewhere together. It would have to be a secret. My dad has some very strict ideas about respecting other people's wishes. But your family's wishes need not be yours. Like I said, it was great fun talking to you. People like you aren't shy. I look forward to hearing from you. Tony Barras.*

P.S. You needn't worry that my dad might read your letter—he never reads letters not addressed to him. That's something else he's very strict about. And a good job too!

Appleby read uninterrupted. When she finished, she got up from the floor and put the note carefully away in the inner pocket of her shoulder bag. Pity I can't write back, she thought, but that really *would* land me in trouble.

It took a day and a half of sheer boredom for Appleby to go back on her sensible decision to ignore the note. Pilbeam was still annoyed with her for talking to Tony in the record shop. They were very cool toward each other these days.

I could write to him, Appleby thought, it would not be such a bad thing to do. If I don't reply at all, he might come here again, and I might not be there to cover his tracks. That would surely be worse than writing a careful answer. Besides, it would be more fun than anything else I have to do.

Dear Tony, she wrote, *I would have replied straight-away to your letter, but I have to be very cautious. Your father is right—my family do not mix with outsiders. We are personages of royal blood, descendants of a deposed European line which I would not even dare to name. Breathe not a word of this to anyone. Destroy this note as soon as you have read it. I know you won't betray me. There are so few people in this world that I can trust, but I am sure I can trust you.*

As for meeting you, that would be very difficult. Write to me again. But do not put your letter in the letter-box. It was sheer luck that I picked it up and not some other member of the household. All letters coming into this house are censored. So we shall need a secret post-box. There is a deep cleft between the bricks just to the right of our gatepost. If you wish to write to me, leave your letter there. I shall look out of the landing window each evening at seven. If I see a light go on and off three times in quick succession at your house, I shall know that there is a note in the wall for me. That would be really interesting. Being a member of a royal house can be pretty boring. Your friend, Appleby Mennym.

Appleby wrote Tony's name and address on the envelope, put a stamp on it, and waited her chance to sneak out to the post-box. This was not the easiest of undertakings. It was not just that she was not supposed to leave the house. There was the more difficult problem of making sure that Pilbeam should suspect nothing. Every time the coast seemed clear, Pilbeam would somehow be there.

"Are you watching me?" said Appleby crossly. "I can't seem to move without your being there."

"Is there anything to watch?" said Pilbeam. "You promised me there would be no more outings till Granpa was satisfied it was safe. You know the danger we were nearly in last time."

"I said no more outings and I meant no more outings," said Appleby. It all depended what one called an "outing." If it meant a trip to the shops or the Market, Appleby would keep her promise, well, for the time-being anyway. Going out after dark to post a letter did not count. And eventually she managed to do it. She was not even detected when she came back.

A few days later, the light in an upstairs room at Number 1 flashed off and on three times in rapid succession. A line of communication had been established. Appleby hurried down to the garden gate and drew her letter from between the stones.

"What are you doing out here?" demanded Tulip as she saw her granddaughter returning up the path. "You are not supposed to be out at all."

"I haven't been anywhere," said Appleby. "The house was stifling. I just wanted a breath of fresh air, Granny. I bet that's why you are out here too."

It was true, and bright of Appleby to realize it. Granny Tulip always did like the evening air.

"We'd better both go in now," said Tulip. "Your mother will be none too pleased if she thinks you're missing." And like two old friends, they went into the house together.

Appleby went straight up to her room, closed the door behind her, put the letter in her bedside drawer and got ready for bed. If Pilbeam came in, she would see Appleby sitting up in bed reading a magazine and would never suspect the letter hidden inside.

Dear Appleby, Tony wrote, *I loved your letter. I don't know how much of it was true, or how much fantasy, but it made interesting reading. And don't worry. I have destroyed it as you asked.*

I hope we manage to think up some way of meeting again. Could you not sneak away and come round to my house some time? My dad is going away for a day or two, something to do with his new job, and my great-aunts go to bed very early. We could listen to records and have a meal together, well, a sort of meal. Do you like Chinese takeaways? Think about it and let me know. It would have to be next Tuesday or Wednesday.

I am going back to school in Harrogate in a fortnight's time, but we could still meet during the holidays. I really would like to get to know you better. No need to bother with the post for your reply. Just leave your note in the cleft in the wall. That's quicker and quite handy. I'll check it every evening after seven.

Please write soon, love, Tony

Appleby read the letter two or three times over. She

was not sure whether to be annoyed with him for doubting her story, but on consideration she decided that since it was fantasy anyway it was not really necessary for her to be indignant. At least he was not asking for the truth, the whole truth and nothing but the truth! There were times when Appleby could be very practical.

The invitation was something else. Appleby had heard of Chinese takeaways. Eating with chopsticks might make a good pretend. But Tony was a human being and he would not understand about pretends.

Dear Tony, wrote Appleby, *It was lovely of you to think I might be able to come and have a meal at your house and listen to your records. It made me realize all over again just how much of a prisoner I am. To come to your home would be impossible. If we are to continue as friends, it can only be as secret penfriends. But even that can be fun.*

Tell me about your school in Harrogate. Do you like going there? Do you play cricket and go rowing on the river? Are you clever at exams and things? I have never been allowed to take any exams. We have a governess called Miss Quigley. She is very strict. My grandfather thinks highly of her because she has an Oxford degree and speaks seven languages. Myself, I would much prefer to go away to school.

Please write again. Love, Appleby

P.S. Very important—don't forget to destroy this letter. I would be in terrible trouble if anyone found out.

The friendship flourished—seven letters in as many days—but there was, of course, no hope of any meeting. When Tony left for Harrogate, Appleby's feelings were mixed. She would miss the excitement of sending and receiving letters. And she was beginning to feel a genuine attachment for Tony. But secrets can be wearing after a while, especially when they involve so much effort. Pilbeam seemed always to be on watch.

9

The Errand-girl

"**Y**ou can tell her to get me another ream of paper, same as the last. And a few more books of postage stamps won't come in wrong," said Sir Magnus.

It was the Thursday after Easter and Tulip had come to see what items she should put on Miss Quigley's weekly shopping list. This was the big one. Other days of the week Miss Quigley was sent as required for odds and ends. Wool, of course, was an entirely separate item with a shopping expedition all to itself. Miss Quigley was very ignorant about wool and Tulip had to give her most specific instructions.

Downstairs in the kitchen, Vinetta was ordering soap powder and a new pair of scissors.

"Don't buy the cheap ones in the Market, Hortensia," she said. "The Market's good for most things, but not scissors. Go to the hardware store in Albion Street, next to Woolworth's."

Poopie came in from the garden and, seeing Miss Quigley all ready in her outdoor clothes, he said, "Is Miss Quigley going shopping?"

"You know she is," said his mother. "She always goes shopping on a Thursday. This is her big shopping day. What do you want?"

Poopie went on talking to his mother as if Miss Quigley needed an interpreter.

"Can she get me four new batteries? Longlife, HP11s." On further thought he added, "I'd better give her a dud one to take with her. Otherwise she's sure to get it wrong."

Miss Quigley gave him a very severe look, but said nothing.

The list went on. Even Joshua added a request.

"Ask her to pop into the cobbler's. My black shoes need heeling. Rubber not leather."

And finally, just as Miss Quigley was on her way to the front door carrying two large shopping bags, Wimpey came rushing out of the playroom.

"Please, Miss Quigley," she said, "if I give you my pocket money, would you bring me a surprise?"

Miss Quigley looked bewildered.

"I wouldn't know what to bring," she said.

"Anything," said Wimpey, looking up at her eagerly. "Anything at all."

"I don't think I can do that," said Hortensia, giving real thought to the child's request. "I might bring something you don't like and then your pocket money would be wasted."

"When Mum did the shopping she often brought me

56

surprises and I always liked them. I like everything. Honest I do."

Hortensia looked at Wimpey's earnest little face and accepted the commission, albeit reluctantly.

When she went out, the treacherous April sky was promising the blessing of a bright Spring day. By the time she came home it was drizzly, windy and miserable. The bags were full and heavy. Miss Quigley, as usual, had procured every item on the list. It had taken her the best part of four hours, going from one shop to another in scattered parts of the town.

"You're a marvel," said Vinetta. "I don't know what we'd do without you."

She took the bulging bags from her and helped her out of her damp coat. Then they both went into the lounge where Wimpey was already waiting.

"It's in the brown bag," said Miss Quigley with a wan smile.

Wimpey carefully unpacked the bag until she came to a box that was clearly meant for her. Trembling fingers opened the "surprise."

"That's super, Miss Quigley," said Wimpey, giving her an unexpected hug. "That little piano's just the right size for my ship."

Miss Quigley sat in the lounge recovering. It was embarrassing to be praised so much, especially when she had made up her mind to resign. On the long walk home she had given it much thought. The heavy bags made it impossible to carry her umbrella. She had stood in a shop doorway and struggled to put a rain-square over her hat, but the rain had trickled uncomfortably down the creases in the plastic and soaked right into her neck. This awful discomfort, added to weeks of forbearance, and feeling exploited, finally drove her to make a very difficult decision. Now Vinetta had to be told. They would all have to be told. And the telling gave Hortensia no joy.

"I am sorry, Vinetta," she said. "I really am sorry, but I can't go on. When I came here, it was as nanny to Baby Googles. I am not a nanny any more. I am a general dogsbody and I've had enough."

Vinetta looked sharply at her friend. She suddenly knew what was coming next and she couldn't bring herself to believe it.

"Today was my last day, my dear," said Hortensia. "I'm not working here any more. I'm returning to my little house in Trevethick Street. I have already written to my friend Maud to tell her I will be coming. I hope you will still allow me to visit you from time to time. And I do hope we will always be friends. But enough is enough."

Soobie, in his seat by the bay window, listened and felt respect for the stand she was taking, even if it did mean her going back to the daftest of all pretends.

"Please Hortensia," Vinetta protested, laying a hand on her friend's arm, "you cannot mean it. You've been happy here. I'm sure something could be done to put things right."

"Say no more, Vinetta," said Miss Quigley, drawing herself up stiff and straight. "I have given it a lot of thought. Nothing you can say will make me change my mind."

She went off to pack, leaving Vinetta to sit and consider what, if anything, she should do. There was no way she could deny her friend the right to return to her old home, a pretend that for forty years had seemed a reality.

"If you could store my art things in the attic," said Miss Quigley as she prepared to go, "I would be most obliged. I will try to think of some way to dispose of them later. Naturally you are welcome to keep any pictures you might like."

Vinetta said nothing. It was so distressing that it should come to this, and so embarrassing. Hortensia, as usual, misinterpreted the silence.

"I wouldn't ask," she said, "but I won't have room for much in Trevethick Street. It is very full already and I would hate to part with any of my father's furniture."

Vinetta could not bring herself to say anything to contradict Hortensia's pretend. Pretends in her eyes were sacred, no matter what. And there was another reason for holding back, one much less spiritual. If she goes, thought Vinetta, it might bring Magnus to his senses. He will be deprived of his supply line.

But the going was sad, very sad. For Trevethick Street was one colossal pretend. Miss Quigley's only other residence was, in truth, the hall cupboard. For forty years she had sat there on a cane-backed chair, coming once a fortnight or so on pretend visits to Brocklehurst Grove. She would sneak out through the kitchen, and come round from the back door to the front.

The bell would ring.

"I wonder who that can be," Vinetta would say.

"It's Miss Quigley," Soobie would reply. "You know perfectly well who it is."

Hortensia Quigley had come a long way since those

days. She had become the perfect nanny to Baby Googles. She had become a very talented artist. For her to return permanently to Trevethick Street was nothing short of tragic.

But there was no other way. No other possibility suggested itself. Hortensia packed her personal belongings into her weekend bag. She took one last look at her beautiful bedroom. Then she went downstairs and, for the first time in over three years, she opened the door to the long cupboard under the stairs in the hall and stepped inside.

They will forget me till I come and visit, she thought. Out of sight is out of mind.

❧ 10 ❧

The Family at Number 9

The Fryers would have claimed to be happily married. But not in the normal, conventional way. Alec and Loretta spent as much time apart as they did together. They were totally faithful and scrupulously loyal; but they had their own lives to lead and they had never allowed marriage or parenthood to interfere with work. They enjoyed one another's company when rest times or holidays brought them together, but when work drew them apart each was slightly relieved to go back to what they thought of as real life.

Over the years, first Tristram and then Anthea had become keepers of the family home, parents to ambitious "children" who went away but came back frequently for long and lovely holidays. Alec and Loretta needed this home-base. It was the reverse of normal, but for many years it had worked perfectly. Now things were about to change. Loretta had decided to retire, and Alec was working on a scheme for country living that might or might not work out. "At least we can give it a try," he said. "Nothing venture, nothing win."

Anthea was kept informed, but *her* wishes were not consulted. They never had been. It was unnecessary. She was a very docile daughter, totally different from her public image. To outsiders she appeared to be a fighter, a strong supporter of deserving causes. It was, maybe, a sort of sublimation of the anger she felt deep down at being the one who stayed at home and did nothing of any importance. That, too, was about to change.

The parents, like dutiful children, wrote letters home from time to time. Alec and Loretta had spent six weeks in residence at Number 9 from mid-February till the end of March. Anthea had introduced Bobby Barras, but her parents were too busy to take any real interest at the time. He would become an afterthought in a letter home, perhaps not even that. Loretta was in London now, working and practicing for her final engagements. Alec had returned to Scotland to house-hunt in real earnest. The letters duly arrived.

Dear Anthea, (wrote Loretta)
    I am writing this on a glorious morning sitting on a seat in Kensington Gardens. How anyone can ac-

cuse April of being a cruel month, for whatever symbolic reasons, I simply do not know. No matter how old I am, I will always feel young when April comes.

But you, my dear, really are young. Now that the gallery's closed, you seem to have so little to be young about. It worries me. Please don't end up married to a widower and living in life's suburbs. Find some real interest, darling, and cut loose. That is something you must do yourself. I cannot make you do it, and I cannot do it for you.

Your father tells me that we will be moving to a moated grange somewhere in the West of Scotland. It will probably suit me. I can play the piano with all the windows open and not feel the least bit guilty! We shall all become country folk—if you'll agree. I am not stupid, Anthea. Your life is your own. We do make plans that include you, but only because you never seem to make any plans for yourself. You must never feel trapped. Too much of my own childhood was spent in feeling trapped.

Love,
Mother

Anthea put the letter into an orange folder with M for Mother scrawled on the flap. She always filed her parents' missives very carefully. She did not fail to notice Mother's oblique reference to Bobby. If she waited for her mother to approve of a suitor she would never marry anyone!

The hint about the "moated grange" made her turn with interest to her father's latest letter.

Dear Anthea, (he wrote)

An Englishman's home they say is his castle. Well, I've bought one. It's not quite a castle and it isn't in England. But I know you'll love it. It is near the West Coast of Scotland with breathtaking views of the Irish Sea. The nearest village is over a mile away. We can become real people in a setting like that. It is truly wonderful.

I shall be returning to Castledean on the twentieth of May, got to go across to Edinburgh first to do a bit more filming, not relishing it. We should have been finished a week ago. By the time I do return, all sorts of arrangements will have been made. We want to get back to the simple life as far as possible, but I couldn't expect Connie or your mother to go primitive on the housework. The plumbing and the wiring need updating. So there'll be a considerable amount of refurbishing to do. It'll be a case of staying on at Brocklehurst till the lease runs out. Good job we didn't buy it. By the autumn, our home, our real home, will be ready.

I hope you're looking forward to it, Petal. I'm sorry the gallery failed, but it was probably all for the best. Things usually do turn out for the best in the long run. You'll enjoy the country. You can get involved in things down in the village, take an active interest, probably end up as a farmer's wife, I shouldn't wonder! Married into a Scottish clan!

Take care of yourself,

Love,
Dad

Anthea smiled as she folded the letter. They would be together at last, these wayward parents. They would become homemakers, belated nest-builders. And she, after all these years, could leave them to get on with it. It would be an enormous relief.

She looked out of the window at the statue of Matthew James in all his civic splendor. She hoped there would be a Brocklehurst Grove in Huddersfield. She was looking forward to being a suburban housewife with children of her own. Bobby Barras was moving to a new job in September, a new job in a new town. And before the year was out, he and Anthea would be married. She had not told the parents yet. Time enough for that when they both came home.

The Great Aunts at Number 1 knew all about their nephew's plans. They were very old, well past the age of interfering or holding on. They looked forward to Bobby's departure as the beginning for them of a quiet time and things being as they used to be. A housekeeper did most of the cooking and all the housework. A man about the house was an intrusion. A boy, if only at holiday times, was an irritation. A pity Bobby's first wife died! A good job he'd found himself another before it was too late.

The Mennyms would have been relieved if *they* had known of Anthea's imminent departure. But they didn't.

11

A Stormy Conference

A conference was held in Granpa's room on Saturday evening. Miss Quigley was not there. She had not appeared for more than a week. Soobie had posted his grandfather's letters at midnight in the letter-box by the old church. No parcels or packages had been sent out. No one had done any shopping.

Vinetta had made the rounds of the family telling them of Miss Quigley's resignation as soon as the cupboard door closed.

"Miss Quigley has decided to go back to Trevethick Street," she said. "I can't say I blame her. We have treated her very badly. And I have been just as bad as the rest of you."

"We haven't enjoyed the past few weeks either, you know," said Tulip. "In a war, we must all pull our weight."

"It isn't a war," Vinetta protested. "It's supposed to be some sort of siege. If you ask me, it's nothing but a ghastly pretend and we are fools for going along with it."

Tulip pursed her lips and gave her daughter-in-law a magisterial look of disapproval.

"It's not," she said, "but even if it were, what right have you to undermine it? One rule for us, another for you and Hortensia Quigley!"

Magnus was even more unpleasant in his criticism.

"You encouraged her," he said. "She hasn't the guts to make a decision on her own. Don't think I can't see through you, Vinetta. You think we'll go back to the game of Russian roulette just because we've nobody who can go outdoors in safety."

"Russian roulette?"

"That's what it would be," said Magnus. "You go to the Market—and, bang, you're dead. Or if it's not you it will be Pilbeam or Appleby. You'll get careless. You'll be seen and cornered. Then it'll be no good crying over spilled milk, madam. It's a dangerous world out there."

"So what do we do?" said Vinetta, keeping her voice level.

"We do without," said Magnus. "No shopping means no purchases. Soobie can take care of the post."

The other members of the family had little to say and looked embarrassed or uncomfortable. It rather depended upon how finely tuned their consciences were.

Vinetta's next ploy was to disappear for hours on end into the nursery to look after Baby Googles. The washing and ironing were totally neglected. Buttons that came off were not sewn on. Quarrels were not resolved by motherly intervention. Vinetta, behind the nursery door, could hear voices raised and shouts for her to come and give judgment as to who was right and who was wrong. She ignored them. Someone had to look after Googles. The poor baby no longer had a nanny.

This would have been a war indeed—a war of attrition—if it had not been for the matches. It would have taken much longer for the conference to be called—if it had not been for the matches . . .

The gas-fires in the Mennym household were well-constructed but rather aged. They were regularly cared for, and cleaned twice a year by Joshua. Being so old, each one had to be lit with a match. It was on Friday morning that Tulip discovered that there was only one box of matches left.

"Someone will *have* to go shopping," she said. "Decisions will have to be made. We shall have to have a conference. We can't go on like this."

So the next day the family gathered in Granpa's room and waited for wisdom.

Magnus looked directly at Vinetta, knowing that she was his chief opponent. He couldn't count the number of times she had argued discreetly and privately that the "siege" should be considered over and that life should be allowed to return to normal.

"Since Miss Quigley's desertion," said Magnus, "we have lost our facility for dealing with the mundane matters of the outside world."

"Miss Quigley is not a facility," said Vinetta.

"I choose my words as carefully as I can, daughter-in-law, but if my level of erudition is not as high as yours, you must bear with me," said Sir Magnus loftily. "To rephrase, in very plain English, we need somebody to go to the shops. Miss Quigley is still the safest person to undertake that task in these troubled times."

"Miss Quigley is not available. She is gone. She does

not live here anymore," said Vinetta. "We have driven her away."

Magnus gave Vinetta a very benign, conciliatory look.

"We did overwork Miss Quigley," he agreed. "Some thoughtless members of this family took advantage of her, used her to run unnecessary errands, even within the house itself. That was disgraceful. Some members of this family began to treat her like a skivvy. It must never happen again."

Vinetta steeled herself for what was coming. But the wily old man addressed Tulip instead.

"You must tell Miss Quigley to come out of the hall cupboard and shop for the necessities. Necessities only."

Vinetta was furious. Magnus had broken every rule in the book.

"How dare you!" she said. "How dare you! Miss Quigley, Hortensia, my friend Hortensia, has gone home to Trevethick Street. She is entitled to go home to Trevethick Street. She came here as a nanny. If and when she returns, it will be as nanny to my baby. Nothing else."

"She's not your puppet," said Magnus, voice raised, black eyes bulging.

"And she's certainly not *yours!*"

Appleby and Pilbeam regarded their mother with a new admiration. They felt like joining in but they had the sense to say nothing. Vinetta was doing very well on her own. The younger twins gaped. Soobie was a silent, satisfied spectator. Joshua, on the stiff-backed seat by the door, looked as if he would like to escape. As for Tulip, she was visibly horrified. No one ever spoke to Sir Magnus Mennym in that tone of voice.

It took some moments for Magnus to recover. Then he said lamely, "Someone has to do the shopping. It doesn't do itself."

"I shall do the shopping," said Vinetta. "Pilbeam will do the shopping. Appleby will do the shopping. Everyone will go back to normal. The siege, if it ever was a siege, is over."

Sir Magnus glowered.

"Then Miss Quigley won't be needed—and she won't be welcome either," he said. "She can stay in Trevethick Street and see how she likes it after the years she's spent with us."

Everyone in the room looked at Vinetta, wondering what she would say next.

She drew a deep breath.

"You are a spiteful old man," she said. "I won't allow it. If I can persuade Hortensia to return to her post as Googles's nanny, then I shall most certainly do so. If she will agree to come back, I shall consider myself very fortunate."

Tulip looked about to argue, but she felt her powers diminishing as Vinetta's grew. She could not risk a conflict in such a public forum. Defeat would be too humiliating.

Sir Magnus's flowing mustache drooped. His face took on an exaggerated look of weariness.

"Do whatever you like," he said. "But go now. I am an old man. I need my rest. I have warned you of the perils. I can do no more."

Pilbeam and Appleby looked at one another. No one else in the room knew about their visit to *Sounds Easy*. No one must ever know. Pilbeam felt guilty. Appleby, with much more to hide, felt not so much guilty as worried about the possibility of being found out.

That evening the sisters went cautiously to the late-night supermarket and bought some matches. The next day they celebrated the return of freedom with a trip to the quayside market. As they walked home up Sandy Bank toward the High Street, the sun was shining and it felt good to be out on a fine April morning.

"We'll just have to be careful," said Pilbeam, thinking of their guilty secret, "more careful than ever."

It was not easy for Pilbeam. She wanted to warn the others, but she feared that to give such a warning might return them to a state of siege. People who are totally honest find compromise very painful. Had she known the full story of Appleby's letters to Tony Barras she would have been horrified.

✤ 12 ✤

The Invitation

It was the May Day Bank Holiday. Appleby and Pilbeam decided to go for a walk. The weather was bright but breezy. They were strolling along the High Street, expecting nothing in particular to happen, when Pilbeam suddenly said, "Don't look now, but there's that boy from Number 1. I think he might have spotted us. Hurry. Hurry this way."

They were beside the Theatre Royal. Appleby found herself being pulled quite roughly round the corner into Kyd Street. She shook herself free. Turning her head to look behind her, she saw Tony watching them and she waved him away frantically. Pilbeam, leading on into the alley, did not suspect a thing. It was enough that the boy from *Sounds Easy* seemed to be noticing them.

"Walk more quickly," she said, "and don't look back,"

When they were well away from danger, up one street and down another, they slowed down and Pilbeam said, "That was a near thing. We really will have to be more careful."

"I thought he'd gone back to school," said Appleby, then stopped in terror as she realized that she might have given herself away.

"What do you mean?" said Pilbeam. "Where did you get that bit of information?"

Appleby, struggling to recover, and managing as usual, said, "The day I spoke to him in the shop, he said he was home for the holidays and would be returning to school in Harrogate or somewhere after Easter."

"Maybe he's just having a long weekend for the Bank Holiday then," said Pilbeam. "Let's hope so. I wish to goodness you'd never spoken to him."

That evening, Appleby went eagerly to look out of the landing window at seven o'clock. With a tingle of excitement she saw a light flash on and off three times at Number 1. Tony was still at home, and he had sent her a letter. Now that the rules were relaxed, going to the front gate was no problem. The excuse that she wanted to breathe in the evening air would hold again if any were needed.

And to take the note from the wall was no great task for Appleby with whom the hand could always be relied upon to be swifter than the eye.

It was over three weeks since she had last heard from Tony. He honorably destroyed all her letters. She kept his in a small cardboard box in the bottom of her wardrobe. This new missive would join the others as soon as she had read it half a dozen times.

Dear Appleby, said Tony, *I wish your sister had not been with you today. It would have been such a good chance to talk. I am home for a week because the school is holding some sort of conference for teachers. What is more, I have tickets for the under-eighteens disco at the Plaza on Saturday. There's a live group playing—The Empty Vessels. They call themselves that because they reckon they can make more noise than any other band. Surely there's some way you could manage to go? Sneak away. I can meet you at the end of the street, or anywhere you like. It's too good a chance to miss. When I go back to Harrogate again I'll be away till the end of July. They're putting an extra week onto the term to make up for missing this one. Please come to the disco. We can have a marvelous time. Leave a message in the wall. Love, Tony*

It would not be Appleby's first disco. She had even been to a disco at the Plaza. It was one of the challenges she had set herself after watching the pop program on TV. The first time she went she had been very nervous. She had nearly turned back at the entrance when she saw two tuxedo-suited doormen standing there looking menacing, but the music drifting out was loud, familiar and friendly.

She had paid at the door on that occasion. Once in the crowd, she was a careful watcher, leaning on the chrome rail near the bar at first so that she could look down on the whole hall. Young people danced alone and ignored each other. Smoke swirled and rainbow lights flickered. A glitter ball made up of hundreds of pieces of mirror rotated up above, catching the lights and making patterns on the dance floor. Appleby had taken courage and danced just like everybody else. It was possible to be a stranger in a crowd like that and never be noticed. But to go there with Tony was surely too great a risk. Then she would not be alone in the crowd. It was impossible. For any normal rag doll it was impossible. But Appleby? Well . . . maybe not.

If I arranged to see him inside, she thought, I could ask him to leave my ticket in the wall. I'd tell him I'd see him beside the pinball machine to the left of the bar. That way he'd know I'd been there before. He wouldn't be suspicious. Then, if things should become difficult after we met inside, I could easily slip away in the crowd and beat a safe retreat behind the pillars.

So there was a warm letter of acceptance in the cleft in the wall. Tony smiled when he read it. Just as his father had a loving tolerance of Anthea's foibles, so Tony could see that there was something about Appleby that did not ring true, but it did not make him like her any the less. She was like no other girl he had ever known. Her secrecy, whether necessary or not, added a piquancy to their friendship.

Appleby took the ticket from the wall and hid it in the pocket of her shoulder bag. The next day she sneaked off alone to *Seconds Galore,* a shop in Rothwell Close, just off the High Street, which specialized in secondhand clothing for young people. Rummaging round, she managed to find a long black skirt with a deep fringe round the hem, a shocking pink top with long sleeves that ended in a point, and a richly-patterned tapestry waistcoat. They were considerably cheaper than they would have been anywhere else, but it still took every penny she had with her, and a bit of haggling, for her to buy them. The assistant paid no attention at all to the butterfly sunglasses and the candy-striped gloves that Appleby did not remove even to pay for her purchases. The assistant had purple hair, a small tattoo on her chin, a ring through her nose, and very strict views about people being free to do their own thing.

Appleby's next task would be to think up some stratagem for escaping from the house, and, more specifically, from Pilbeam when Saturday came.

I can pretend to be tired and say I am going to bed early. I can quarrel with her about something and go in the sulks. Appleby lay on her bed late into the night just wondering what to tell Pilbeam. Nobody else mattered. Nobody else watched her the way Pilbeam did. Nobody else was as suspicious.

"Drat it!" said Appleby out loud and she dug a fist into her pillow. What can I tell her? Her mind came back with a surprising answer. Tell her the truth. A lie won't do this time. Tell her a half-truth anyway.

"Pilbeam," said Appleby in a little, secret voice, "if I tell you something will you promise not to tell the others?"

She was sitting on the chair in Pilbeam's room, having

74

disturbed her sister's sleep at a quarter past midnight. One rule for Appleby, another for everybody else!

"I'm making no promises," said Pilbeam, trying to wake up. "For all I know you might be deciding to run off somewhere. And if you are, I will tell! Simple as that."

"No!" said Appleby. "It's nothing like that. Do you think I'm stupid or something? Everything's back to normal. We go out shopping. We could even go to the pictures if we wanted to, or the theater, or a concert like you said we could. There's no reason to run away."

Pilbeam thought Appleby's idea that they would be free to lead a richer, fuller life than ever was a bit optimistic, but the argument served its purpose. It minimized what Appleby really intended to do and it put Pilbeam off her guard.

"Very well then," said Pilbeam. "Tell me your secret. I won't tell the others, but I will give you my opinion."

"Do you think it's possible," said Appleby, "for me to go out somewhere after dark, like Soobie does? Well, not quite dark, more like dusk really? I mean to say Soobie goes out at times when I just wouldn't dare. But then he's a boy. Girls can't expect to have as much freedom."

Appleby cleverly mentioned the one thing calculated to make Pilbeam's hackles rise. Boys and girls, men and women, should be treated equally in all respects. To quote Granpa, who sometimes said things he did not strictly mean, what was sauce for the goose should be sauce for the gander.

"I can't imagine you wanting to go jogging," said Pilbeam, "but I suppose if you did you should have as much right to do so as Soobie. Though, of course, Soobie is rather special, being blue. He can't go out during the day.''

"Of course I don't want to go jogging," said Appleby derisively. "That would be *far* too dangerous for me. I don't know how Soobie *dares* do it."

"All right then, what do you want to do?"

"Well, you remember the other day I bought a new pair of boots at that little shop in the High Street?"

Pilbeam nodded but wondered where this side-track was leading. She remembered her sister coming back with the boots. She knew the little shop well. It was one they often used, being not too well lit. The assistants were two fussy but rather nice old women who thought that all teenagers looked weird with their punky clothes and hairdos, and goodness knows where they got the money from! Still, Florrie used to say to Joyce, they spend it here and that's the main thing—and them boots aren't so bad, you know, better than the winkle-pickers we wore when we were young.

"You'll never guess what those two in the shop are doing now," said Appleby. "They've got a promotion on, giving away tickets for the disco at the Plaza. I could hardly believe it. Everybody who spent more then ten pounds on boots last week was given a ticket. And I got one."

"I don't believe you," said Pilbeam.

"It's true," said Appleby, "absolutely true. Look, here's the ticket."

Pilbeam looked at the ticket and then said, "But you're not going."

"Yes, I am," said Appleby. "Just for a short time. I've done it before. You know I have."

"That was a long time ago," said Pilbeam.

"Not more than five years. It won't have changed much. It's just like I told you—lights and smoke and heavy-metal music. You wouldn't like it. But I don't have to like everything you like. I wouldn't have gone to see *The Merchant of Venice*. You did. And I'll only stay for an hour. You can be my ally. You can make sure nobody here finds out I've gone. And you can be on the look out for me coming back. It's harmless, honestly it is."

Pilbeam looked uncertain. Now was the right time for Appleby to lose her temper. It was an old technique she had for pushing people to her side of the fence.

She stood up and said, "All right, all right. I won't go. I'll tear the ticket up. I never get anywhere. And I don't even get dressed up in posh clothes like you do. I've got no life at all. I wish I'd been a boy."

"Sit down," said Pilbeam. "We'll talk about it."

"What's the point?" said Appleby, but she sat down all the same. "You don't want me to go. So I won't go. End of subject."

"It's not up to me," said Pilbeam. It was late and she was tired.

"Yes it is," said Appleby. "If you go and tell Mum or Granny, I'll be in trouble. It's easy for you to stop me doing anything."

"All right," said Pilbeam. "Go to the disco for an hour, if that's what you want. But if you are not back by half past ten I'll have to tell Mum. If you're not back by eleven o'clock we'll all be petrified. And that wouldn't be fair."

Appleby rose from her seat and went over and hugged her sister.

"You're fantastic," she said. "You're the best sister anybody could have. And I promise you faithfully I'll be back in this house by twenty past ten, if not sooner. It's no big thing, you know. Just a little jaunt."

13

The Visitor

Vinetta had too much respect for Hortensia to dash straight to the hall cupboard and tell her the outcome of the conference. Her sense of decorum demanded that she should wait till Miss Quigley in kid gloves, felt hat and neat brown suit, should, of her own accord, decide to pay her friend a visit.

It was on Wednesday morning after the Bank Holiday that the cupboard door opened and Miss Quigley stepped out, closed the door quietly behind her and made her way through the kitchen to the back of the house.

Joshua had just come in from the garden and was removing the gloves he always wore for weeding. He spread out a sheet of newspaper and carefully brushed the soil off them. Very deliberately, he kept his back to Miss Quigley and gave not the slightest hint that he had seen her pass by. That was the way it had always been done in the old days, before the visitor had become the nanny. In those days, everyone in the family had supported this pretend. Between the cupboard and the back door, the visitor must be invisible and all who might see her must keep their eyes averted.

The front doorbell rang and Soobie, seeing the visitor through the window, called in the friendliest of voices, "Miss Quigley's at the door, Mother."

This was not Soobie's usual way. In the old days, as he sat in the chair by the window, he would have been very scathing about the pretend visit from the woman who really lived in the cupboard. But the wise blue Mennym, old head on young shoulders, knew that this visit was a first and a last. Things would return to normal. Miss Quigley would once again make her home in Brocklehurst Grove and resume her duties as nanny to Googles.

"What a lovely surprise!" said Vinetta as she opened the front door. "We have all missed you, especially the baby. If I weren't such a sensible woman, it would have made me quite jealous. She looks so pathetic, poor lamb, and keeps asking for her 'nanna.'"

Miss Quigley smiled politely, but there was frost in the air.

"And how are things in Trevethick Street?" asked Vinetta as they settled in the lounge with the tray, as of old, on the coffee table in front of them. Vinetta poured imaginary liquid into the willow-patterned tea cups.

"Trevethick Street never changes," said Miss Quigley. "Life goes on as usual. My neighbor, Miss Whiteley, has been keeping an eye on things. And, of course, you will remember my telling you that little Lotus Turner adopted my cat. The windows needed cleaning, but that was all.''

Miss Quigley then slipped into another pretend which Vinetta accepted without a murmur. In the world of the Mennyms, contradiction was considered to be in very bad taste.

''It is not as if I have been away so very long,'' said Miss Quigley. ''The occasional weekends I have spent there, and my summer holidays, have kept the house lived in.''

''Still,'' said Vinetta, ''I do think you should have let it to someone. It would have been the practical thing to do. Maybe this time you will give it serious thought.''

''This time?'' Miss Quigley's voice was charged with meaning. Unfriendly, suspicious meaning, tinged with outrage at what might be coming next.

Vinetta understood.

''It's not what you might think, Hortensia,'' she said. ''If you agree to come back, to come *home,* to your own room in this house, no one will ever ask you to do the shopping again. You will be nanny to Googles and that will be the sum total of your duties. This house is no longer under siege. That silly, distressing pretend is over.''

Miss Quigley looked doubtful.

''Please say yes,'' said Vinetta. ''The family feels incomplete without you. I know you have your friends in Trevethick Street. I know that the little house there has been dear to you. But we need you here, Hortensia. Googles needs you. And we all miss you.''

Suddenly, embarrassingly, Miss Quigley began to sob. Her narrow shoulders heaved and fell.

"What is it?" said Vinetta anxiously. "What's wrong, Hortensia?"

Miss Quigley pulled herself together and sat up straight. With a woebegone look she said, "It's just that I thought nobody wanted me. I thought you were all glad to see the back of me. I waited so long for a message inviting me to tea or something. And none came. I thought, maybe they've forgotten me completely."

Vinetta was conscience-stricken.

"How little we understand others!" she said. "I thought you wanted to be alone for a while, to spend some time on your own in Trevethick Street. I didn't want to intrude. Not for the world would I have hurt you like this if I'd known."

Miss Quigley looked at Vinetta and knew that this was the truth.

"I'll come back," she said, regaining her usual composure, "but they must all clearly understand that I am not a servant. I am Googles's nanny, nothing else. I think I would be happier with it written into my contract this time, if you don't mind."

"Of course not," said Vinetta. "I can't say I blame you. Sir Magnus might think he's a gentleman, but he has no idea of what is meant by a gentleman's agreement."

Miss Quigley nodded. She was well pleased with the way things were turning out, but she felt that there was no need for her to express anything that might sound like gratitude.

"Now," said Vinetta, "do let me pour you another cup of tea. Then perhaps you would like to come and see Googles. I know she will be delighted to see *you*."

Throughout this conversation, Soobie had sat unnoticed in his armchair. He still found the silly pretends very irritating, but he was pleased with the conclusion to this one. Rag dolls, he thought, have enough to suffer without causing pain to one of their own kind.

❧ 14 ❧

The Disco

FREE-DOM~~
Freedom-calling, freedom-calling, freedom-calling YOU
COME-OUT~~
In the moonlight, in the starlight, dance the whole night
through

The group produced more decibels per cubic inch than any scientific study of the subject could have promulgated as a hypothesis. In other words, they were whoosh!

"Like it?" asked Tony, shouting down into the red hair that hid Appleby's cloth ear.

Appleby did not attempt an answer but nodded vigorously and clapped to the rhythm. The crowd were not dancing at that moment, just swaying en masse as they stood round the band on the stage. Appleby felt impatient. If they did not return to the floor soon, her chance to dance, really dance, might be missed.

One by one the dancers moved out onto the floor dancing to the rhythm with their own steps in their own private world. And each one danced alone. Appleby reached the center of the floor and, oh, how she danced! First stepping gracefully and then twisting into a jive before returning to the swaying motion of the people round the stage. Then again, step as in a gavotte, twist, jive, bend the music to the steps or the steps to the music, throw in the occasional jesting movement that might have come straight from the ballet. A history of the dance in one lithe dancer. And above her the glitter ball gleamed. Tony danced beside her, a little apart, more simply, with less originality. But he watched his partner and he admired what he saw. Other dancers looked on and some even tried to imitate the redhead in the swirling black skirt who could outdance any dancer on the floor. She was really something!

At a pause in the music, she went with Tony to a table by the bar to rest. People were drinking various soft drinks. Tony asked Appleby what she would like, but she shook her head.

"I never drink anything here," she said. "I am allergic to additives and they don't sell anything that is additive-free. Besides, to be truthful, I am not really thirsty. But don't let me stop you having a drink."

Appleby, like many a Cinderella before her, did not notice the time. The group left the stage for a break and the disc-jockey put on an old record, a really old record, soft and dreamy and sentimental. The lights were lowered to a mere whisper. Tony put out a hand to grasp Appleby's for the first time that evening.

His fingers touched . . . cloth?

"You're wearing gloves," said Tony in surprise. "I never noticed."

He had already wondered why she kept on her mirror sunglasses but had been too polite to ask. Maybe it was just the fashion. Appleby's own style, whatever. Anyone who knew Appleby accepted everything she did as the norm for her. But the gloves were surprising. They looked just like hands. Well, as near as one could see in disco lights.

Appleby was startled. *She was not wearing gloves.* She had drawn away her hand as soon as Tony had touched it, but that might be too late. What on earth could she say? A false hand, lost my hand in America when I was a baby, bitten off by an alligator. Rubbish! Play for time. Yes, *of course* I am wearing gloves. I always wear gloves. Why am I wearing gloves? Play for time . . .

"I could tell you a whole string of lies," began Appleby, clasping her hands together cautiously on the table in front of her, but in such a way that the shadow, of her head concealed them, "—like how my eyes and my hands are photosensitive and have to be protected from the light—and how it's even worse with the dry ice in here. The truth is simpler." And suddenly the simpler story became the truth, or at least the acceptable lie. "I have to take special care of my hands because I am employed by a model agency to advertise creams and lotions. My hands have appeared on TV. The gloves are a thin, transparent covering. I wouldn't dare be without them in a place like this."

"And what about the specs?" asked Tony, not believing a word of it but amused by the lies and encouraged to ask more. If a lie is funny enough the truth ceases to matter.

"I," said Appleby with exaggerated slowness, "am a woman of mystery. That is my style."

Tony grinned.

The sentimental tune ended and a livelier one began.

"Come on then, my woman of mystery, let's give them another demonstration of what dancing *should* be!"

They got up to return to the floor.

Appleby felt the weight and the warmth of Tony's hand on her shoulder as he steered her forward, and she knew it was time to retreat. A much simpler lie this time, simpler and safer.

"I have to go somewhere. I'll not be a minute," she said and whipped off into the crowd. Tony waited. The tune ended but Appleby did not return. Cinderella did not even leave her slipper behind.

The colored lights brightened. The group began to play again. Their lead singer belted out defiant words.

I'm shooting off to
Wherever *I want to, wherever I want to, wherever I want*
To . . . GO, GO, GO!
Think you *can catch me? 'Course you can't catch me.*
No-one can catch
Me . . . NO, NO, NO!

Tony stood alone in the crowd listening, not knowing how true were the words of the song.

* * *

It was a quarter to eleven when Appleby arrived home. Pilbeam was waiting to let her secretly in at the back door. She was not panicking, not yet. She knew Appleby too well to expect her to be spot on time. As for ten minutes early! Fifteen minutes late was certainly not bad.

"Let's go straight to my room and you can tell me all about it," said Pilbeam. So they went quietly up the stairs, pleased to note that the breakfast-room door was closed.

"So you got home safely," said Pilbeam when the two of them were settled in her room.

Appleby did not look as happy as she should have done. She seemed flustered.

"It was wonderful," she said in a tone that firmly contradicted the look on her face. "I've never had such a marvelous time. It was magic."

But she couldn't keep it up. She choked on the words and began to sob.

"Oh, Pilbeam," she said when she was able to speak again, "it was awful. I was having the best time of my life when suddenly being a rag doll mattered. I could stay there no longer without being found out. So I ran away. And I felt so confused I went down the wrong street coming home and almost managed to get lost. I don't like being a rag doll, Pilbeam. I hate it. I hate it. I hate it."

Pilbeam put her arm round Appleby's shoulders.

"Hush," she said. "You don't want the others to hear. Listen to me. I can't change the facts but I can, maybe, teach you to live with them. We are rag dolls. That sets us aside from other thinking beings. But, you could say, it makes us very special. Our life is wonderful because it should not exist at all. *You* are wonderful, Appleby Mennym. *You* are magic. My real time with you has been so short, no matter what my fictional imagination might supply as a past. And in that real time I have learned not only to love you but to admire your verve and your zest for life. You are a very important member of this family. We would be the poorer without you. Accept what you are, Appleby, and go on being as you are.''

She stroked Appleby's hair, her head being bent to hide her face. They sat silent for some minutes. Then Appleby told Pilbeam everything, all about the letters in the wall and the truth about the disco ticket.

Pilbeam was shocked but managed not to show it. She listened to the whole story and tried to understand.

''It was a terrible risk to take,'' she said when Appleby had finished, ''but it's over now. You might have been found out, but you weren't. What we must do now is gather up the pieces. One more note to be left in the wall, a final farewell. I'm sorry that's how it has to be but time heals and we have more time than most.''

Appleby looked up and said, ''Oh, Pilbeam, what would I do without you? But, it still hurts to think about it. If I were not—not as I am—I could have loved him. His eyes were blue, deep, deep blue and his smile was warm and friendly. And, and, oh, he was fun to be with.''

''I know,'' said Pilbeam. ''I know.''

And she did.

In the calm that followed, they prepared a note to be left in the wall, a sensible, quiet little note in which

Appleby said she was sorry for leaving the disco in such haste (*my brother arrived unexpectedly to take me home and I was unable to find you*) and added that her family had decided to send her abroad for a year. (*So when next you return from Harrogate, I won't be here.*)

They went together to put the note in the cleft in the wall.

Next evening, Appleby sat in the lounge from seven till midnight, watching for Tony to come and look for a message in the wall. Soobie was puzzled at the sadness in his sister's face, but said nothing. When he left the lounge, Appleby moved from the high-backed seat into his armchair. As the long twilight turned to darkness, she became more and more miserable. It was all very well to talk bravely about acceptance. But being brave merely hides the hurt. It does not heal it.

Tony did not appear. He would be returning to Harrogate next morning. Appleby knew that. Would he ever know about the note? Would he care?

Left alone at the disco that evening, Tony had at first felt puzzled, then annoyed. He had returned to the pinball table near the bar, thinking that the sensible thing to do. Then he had walked round the edge of the hall, looking over the chrome rails, just as Appleby had once done. But he could see no sign of his partner. He thought of his own awkward dancing and of her brilliance. Then, remembering all the obvious lies she had ever told him, he realized that he did not really know her at all. She was a stupid girl playing stupid games. That, he thought, as he kicked at a can that lay in his path on the way back home, is the end of it. Let her fool with some other fellow!

But his anger hid the pain of love rejected. Rag dolls are not the only ones who can be hurt.

❧ 15 ❧

A Trip to the Park

The big green perambulator was twenty years old. Vinetta had bought it out of one of Tulip's many catalogues. For the first seventeen years of its life it had been taken no further than the back garden. Vinetta would not have dared to take Googles out into the street in it. Indeed, she had never taken Googles out into the street at all. She had known from the start that babies attract attention even in the most sedate of neighborhoods. It was only after Miss Quigley took over as nanny that the real visits to the real park had begun. For Miss Quigley had perfect faith that her own aura of anonymity, in most conceivable situations, would extend to the baby in the pram.

When Miss Quigley resumed her duties as nanny. one of the first things she did was to set out on a bright May morning to take Googles for a trip to the park. Under the sun canopy, Googles lay propped up against pink silk pillows smiling joyfully and rattling her favorite plastic bear.

Miss Quigley pushed the pram out of the Grove in the opposite direction to the park, a necessary detour if the visit was to be a complete success. She crossed the main road and made her way down the side street that led to the open air Market, which, it being Thursday, bustled with people. Miss Quigley did not go into the Market itself. The perambulator would have been truly conspicuous if any attempt had been made to push it up and down the aisles. The only stall in which Miss Quigley had any interest was a small baker's, on the edge of the complex, where she bought a flat cake of bread. Then, mission accomplished, she headed for the park.

The warmth and the sunshine were enough to attract a few extra visitors, but it was a school day and so there were no schoolchildren. Miss Quigley pushed the pram down the broad path toward the lake. She passed the playground where a few young mothers were concentrating on their own babies and toddlers, pushing swings and turning roundabouts. Next she came to the boathouse where the rowing boats were tied. Beyond that was an enclosure where two goats looked hopefully over a wire fence. Miss Quigley propped Googles up so that she could watch. Then she broke bits off the bread and fed the goats. Googles rocked forward and clapped her hands.

Next they went round to the far side of the lake. It was the turn of the ducks and swans to receive Miss Quigley's benison. Googles, growing braver, stretched over the edge of the pram to watch. Miss Quigley gave her a piece of the bread and helped her to throw it.

"Just look at that greedy one," she said, pointing out a militant mallard that was edging the other birds out of the way to secure the lion's share of the crumbs.

When all the bread was gone, they went on past the tennis courts and through the stone arch that led to the green around the bandstand. Googles, growing tired, lay back and fell asleep. This was the quietest part of the park. Miss Quigley put the brake on the pram, sat down on a sheltered bench, and took out an old paper-backed edition of *Rasselas*. Things were back to normal. Happy days!

At half past eleven precisely, Miss Quigley closed her book and set off for home. She took the long way home, out through the side gate and along the quiet, tree-lined avenue. It was so peaceful that it was hard to believe that the town was less than half a mile away.

But as Miss Quigley approached Brocklehurst Grove and there were more people about, she felt suddenly uneasy, as if she might be noticed after all. It was an unusual, unnerving feeling. In her time as nanny, she had never felt like this before. She walked more quickly and gripped the pram handle more tightly. When she came to Number 5, she took the precaution of entering the gate backward so that the pram hood and the canopy would protect Googles from any curious eyes. Two wheels of the pram were inside the gate, the other two were still on the pavement, when Googles woke up and in a sudden swift movement flung her pink plastic bear to the ground.

"The baby's dropped its rattle," said Anthea Fryer, appearing from nowhere. A startled Miss Quigley reached out a gloved hand, grabbed the bear and said, "Thank you."

"How old is she?" asked Anthea, guessing that the pink canopy hid a baby girl. She came closer, ready to peep under the hood.

Miss Quigley said urgently, "I think you should stay away, dear. Baby has whooping cough."

Googles, fully awake now, heard the words "whooping cough." They triggered off a reaction, awakening a pretend that had lain dormant for over forty years. Googles held her breath for a second, and then gave a very realistic cough culminating in an undeniable whoop. She was not to know that her coughing supported her nanny's urgent lie.

"Poor little thing," said Anthea. "I hope she'll be better soon." Then she hurried away and said no more. That was all there was to it. But that was more than enough.

Miss Quigley entered the house in a state of terror. Only her presence of mind had saved them from inevitable disclosure. But she had told a lie that could backfire and she recognized the danger almost as soon as the words were out of her mouth.

"I thought I was invisible," she said to Vinetta. "Up till today, I genuinely believed that no one ever noticed me."

"The baby at Number 5 has whooping cough." said Anthea to Connie Witherton. "It seems odd that she is being taken out in the street. They are peculiar people. It wouldn't surprise me if they haven't even called the doctor in."

"They must have," said Connie. "It is a notifiable disease. But I don't think that means they have to keep the child indoors. And it is a lovely day. Still, I'll check with my friend Sarah next time she drops in."

Sarah, besides being Connie's friend, was also the local health visitor.

Oh what a tangled web we weave, when first we practice to deceive.

❧ 16 ❧

The Neighbors

*H*ow did they manage it? All those years, undetected, living as if they were a totally ordinary family?

It is not so hard to understand with regard to the world beyond the Grove. Human beings are much too busy with their own affairs to pay much regard to people they don't know. The exceptions are those who, either on purpose or by accident, draw attention to themselves or, in the words of Sir Magnus, raise their heads above the parapet. The Mennyms were past-masters at keeping their heads down.

In the Trevethick Street of Miss Quigley's imagining, neighbors gossiped with each other and kept a more or less friendly eye on the folks next door. But Brocklehurst Grove was at the upper end of the suburban market. The people who lived there were as various as the people who lived anywhere else, but there was a general ambience of uppishness, of feeling that it was not quite proper to hob-nob with the neighbors. Last year's fight to save Brocklehurst Grove had been a real culture shock. Meetings at Number 9 had been attended reluctantly, and support had never reached the hundred percent level.

Jane and Eliza Proud, who lived at Number 1, had sent

their nephew, Bobby, along to every meeting, but had shown no interest whatsoever in what was said there.

"We're too old for all this," they said. "I don't know why we can't be left in peace."

The Richardsons at Number 2 had been more forthcoming because they were more worried. They had moved in only two years before and, even after help from both their families, were paying out on a heavy mortgage. They were a very unusual, quietly idealistic couple—in their mid-twenties, but hoping to spend the next forty years in Brocklehurst Grove, raising a family, giving love to the next generation and the generation after that. They too were relieved when it was all over and they could go back to being on no more than nodding terms with the neighbors. They were not so much unfriendly as genuinely shy, thinking that everyone else in the street was richer and more glamorous and more important than they were.

The owner of Number 3 did not even appear at the meetings. Ebenezer Paris Dingle was a very, very important man, much too important to join in any local activity. His expensive automobile was one of the things that confirmed the Richardsons in their youthful feelings of inferiority. Moving on would present no problem to Ebenezer Paris Dingle. He did not care whether the Grove was demolished or not. He had spent most of his adult life moving on in this shrinking world.

At Number 4 lived the Jarmans. They had resided in the street far longer than any of the others, nearly thirty years in fact. When they had first moved in the postman had put a letter for Sir Magnus Mennym in the wrong door. It seemed an opportunity for the very nice Jarmans to get to know their neighbors. They sent their son, Oswald, to make the delivery. The boy was not really happy about going, but he rang the doorbell, hoping no one would answer. No one did. The letter was put through the Mennym letterbox and Oswald went home.

The Mennyms were not ex-directory. Inertia had given them an entry below Menning and above Menown. Next day, Mrs. Jarman found their number and rang them.

"Yes?" said Sir Magnus who had picked up the phone at his bedside.

"Hello," said Mrs. Jarman. "I am your new neighbor, Millie Jarman. I wonder if you could tell me which day the binmen come? We've such a lot of packaging to get rid of. You know how it is . . ."

Sir Magnus ignored the question, to which he did not in any case know the answer.

"I hope you'll be happy in your new home," he said. "It is a quiet street. No one will trouble you. We all keep ourselves very much to ourselves. That is the best way. Good fences, as they say, make good neighbors."

He put the phone down noisily and that was that. Mrs. Jarman felt rebuffed and embarrassed. She troubled no one else in the street for the next twenty years.

Then the Englands moved into Number 6. Once again a letter was put into the wrong door.

"Yes?" said Mrs. Jarman when she picked up the phone.

"Hello," said little Mrs. England in a flutter. "I'm afraid we've got one of your letters. The postman put it in here by mistake. And I'm awfully sorry but the dog picked it up. It's not destroyed or anything. It's just a bit marked, if you know what I mean."

Mrs. Jarman, who after all these years was still a very nice woman, smiled into the mouthpiece.

"You didn't say your name," she said.

"Gosh, no, I didn't, did I? I'm Wendy, Wendy England. We've just moved into Number 6. Shall I bring your letter round? I'd have put it straight in your box, but I felt I had to explain the marks."

"Come round now if you like," said Mrs. Jarman. "Come and have coffee with me. We'll get to know each other."

And that was how their friendship began.

Number 7 had been home to a succession of tenants, employees of a large company that liked their staff to be mobile. The company owned the house. The tenants were always ready to be moved onward and upward. Nigel and Dorcas Butterfield had lived there for over a year without exchanging a word with anyone in the neighborhood. They occasionally held barbecues in their back garden, but none of the neighbors was ever invited.

The Davidsons had lived at Number 8 for seven years. They kept themselves apart from strangers and were happy, in their own community. Bernie Davidson had attended the protest meetings at Number 9, but it had been difficult. He was an unworldly man, a student of history, with a long sad history of his own. With his wife and children, he had watched from the window as Miss Fryer climbed up to tie the triumphant banner to the chimney of Number 9. The scene to them was incredible. But funny. Bernie smiled a slow smile.

"Well, Becky," he said to his wife, "now I think we have seen everything!"

So seven households could be expected safely to ignore the residents of Number 5. But Anthea Fryer, the sharp-eyed tenant of Number 9, more than made up for the rest.

❧ 17 ❧

In the Nursery

"We mustn't tell any of the others, Hortensia," said Vinetta when she and Miss Quigley had settled on the long sofa in the day nursery. Googles was in her cot watching a fleet of mobile teddy bears turning in the air above her. It was the day after Hortensia's encounter with Anthea Fryer. Mid-afternoon sun streamed through the window which looked out onto the front garden.

"We will be watchful, of course," Vinetta went on, "and Googles will have to be kept indoors. But apart from that, things can go on as they are."

This decision had not been lightly reached. The day before, when Hortensia had come in, hysterical and almost incoherent, Vinetta had put Googles into the cot and had made her nanny go straight to her room to lie down.

"Say nothing," she had said to Hortensia, "not yet. I need time to think."

She had broken the habit of years and not even confided in Joshua.

"If Magnus were to find out," she explained to Hortensia, "it would be back to the siege again, and neither of us wants that! So we keep it to ourselves."

"Won't the others wonder why I never take the baby out?" said Hortensia, trying to make sure that nothing had been overlooked.

"I don't suppose they will even notice," said Vinetta. "But if they do, so what? It is none of their business."

The two women had deliberately withdrawn to the day nursery for their discussion because it was one of the few places in the house where they could hope to sit undisturbed.

"I'm still a bit worried about the lie I told," said Hortensia. "It might have repercussions. Whooping cough is an infectious disease. People get worried about it."

"Where's your mother got herself to now?" Granny Tulip asked Soobie who was in his usual seat at the lounge window.

He looked up from his book and said, "I think she went into the day nursery with Miss Quigley."

Tulip rarely visited the nursery, but she had a sixth sense for something-going-on-that-she-didn't-know-about.

"Well," she said as she came in, "what's been happening today?"

Miss Quigley looked uncomfortable.

Vinetta, totally in control, said, "Pretty much the same as happens every day. Is something wrong?"

"Not as far as I know," said Tulip, looking at Vinetta

over the gold rims of her little spectacles. "I just have this feeling that someone's up to something."

"Well, it's not me," said Vinetta with a smile, "and it's certainly not Hortensia."

At that moment, Googles unfortunately decided to demonstrate her newly discovered talent. She gave a horrendous cough that ended in a very alarming whoop.

"What on earth . .?" said Tulip. "That child sounds as if she has whooping cough."

Vinetta took the offensive.

"Don't get carried away, Tulip. Don't forget what we are. It is another of the perks—Mennyms don't get whooping cough, or any other cough for that matter. We have natural immunity!"

Tulip looked at her suspiciously. Her daughter-in-law had become increasingly independent in her thinking over the past year or two. The family's enforced trip to the country, traumatic for Sir Magnus, had made subtle differences to all of them.

"Why did Googles cough then?" said Tulip, determined to stick to the point.

"It's a pretend," said Vinetta. Hortensia looked on anxiously.

The afternoon sun slanted in through the window and Googles reached for the shadows of the teddy bears as they moved round the paneled side of her cot. Another whoop seemed appropriate, so she made it.

"Where did she get the pretend from?" Tulip insisted. "She's much too young to have thought it up for herself. Something must have put the idea into her head."

Vinetta felt angry. What right had Tulip to pry so?

"I don't know where she got it from," said Vinetta sharply, "and, what is more, I don't care. It is a pretend and in all fairness we must go along with it. My daughter is a very lively baby with a vivid imagination. She has as much right to a pretend as anyone else in the family."

Quarrels in the Mennym household were like movements in music. Vinetta's crescendo was answered by a quiet, contained, but somehow superior lull.

"You are right, of course," said Tulip in an icy little voice that made the opposite sound true. "The hundred days cough, as I believe the Chinese call it. Shall we have a hundred days of baby being ill?"

The sarcasm did not matter. To both Vinetta and Hortensia, the idea sounded utterly brilliant. It was the perfect pretend, the cover they needed to explain their decision to keep Googles safely out of sight.

"And naturally," said Miss Quigley in her best nanny tones, "there will have to be a period of quarantine. We don't want any of the other children catching it."

Tulip, still uneasy, said no more about it.

"It's a lovely day," she said, looking out of the window. "A pity to be stuck indoors. I think I'll take my knitting out into the back garden."

A very tall woman with short, wiry gray hair was striding past the front gate. Tulip noticed her briefly, but without any interest. She was just a stranger passing quickly by. No one in the Mennym household would have recognized Sarah Benson, the health visitor.

18

Intruders

Sarah called in at Number 9 to see her friend, Connie Witherton. They had been at school together and had been overjoyed at their reunion when the Fryers moved into Brocklehurst Grove nearly five years ago.

"My feet are killing me," said Sarah as she sat down in one of Connie's deep armchairs. "I must've walked miles today."

"I've been hoping you'd drop in," said Connie.

"Drop's the word for it," said Sarah as she settled down.

Over the usual coffee cups, Connie told Sarah about Anthea's concern that the baby at Number 5 had whooping cough and might not be receiving proper care and attention.

"I don't suppose there's anything to worry about really, but once Anthea gets a bee in her bonnet it's very hard to budge. I thought things might have been better now she's planning to marry, but old habits evidently die hard."

Sarah did not look unduly worried. From a professional viewpoint, it seemed a small matter. Only friendship would make her give it a second thought.

"People round here tend to be very careful of their offspring," she said, "but I'll see what I can find out, just in case. What's their name?"

"Mennym," said Connie, and then spelled it out. The name, with its curious spelling, had only become known to her at the time of the petition to save Brocklehurst Grove from the planners.

Back at the office, the computer drew a blank when Sarah enquired about patients by the name of Mennym. Early next afternoon, she called and told Connie. Anthea joined them.

"There's definitely something suspicious about that family," she said. "I've known there was from the day we moved here."

That was not strictly true, but at that moment Anthea thought it was.

"We mustn't jump to conclusions," said Sarah. "They may be registered with some doctor out of the area. Or the baby's name might not be Mennym."

Anthea looked stubborn.

"You don't know them the way we do," she said. "There's something very odd about the whole family."

"I'll tell you what," said Sarah, "if it'll make you any happier, I'll go along and introduce myself and make a few polite enquiries. That's the most I can do."

So Sarah, feeling more self-conscious about a visit than she had done for years, found herself walking up the path to the front door of Number 5. She rang the bell. Inside, the unwanted-visitor routine was already in progress.

Soobie had seen the stranger coming through the gate, an official-looking stranger dressed in sober navy that looked almost like a uniform. He rose quickly from his chair and went to the kitchen to find his mother.

"There's a woman coming to the front door," he said. "You'd better get ready to answer."

They had a strategy that had been effective for years and years. Social callers were unknown, but officials who came to the house, such as meter-readers, had to be admitted sometimes and it was always necessary to follow a strict procedure. Reduce visibility, avoid contact, and try to fade into the woodwork. Vinetta put on her tinted spectacles and carefully closed all the doors leading onto the hall. Soobie, on his way to his bedroom, lowered the blind on the landing window. The hall was shrouded in gloom.

The doorbell rang.

Sarah stood on the doorstep waiting, looking curiously to left and right. Like every other house in the street, it looked prosperous, well-cared for, and inviolable. Sarah was about to turn away when the door opened a fraction and a voice said, "Yes?"

Sarah, feeling very wrong-footed, peered in at the doorway. A woman of medium height and build, with dark hair and wearing spectacles, was standing in the shadows, one hand firmly clasped on the front door, her whole attitude saying very clearly, thus far and no further.

"My name's Sarah Benson," said the visitor in a friendly voice. "I am a health visitor in this area. I believe your baby has whooping cough. If there is any help or advice I can offer, please don't hesitate to ask. I know how worrying it can be, especially when the child is so young."

Vinetta gasped. Then panic made her blurt out a desperate denial.

"I don't have a baby," she said. "There are no babies in this house."

It was the last thing Sarah had expected to hear. The existence of a baby at Number 5, suffering from whooping cough, was a well-attested fact as far as she was concerned. Had Vinetta said that Doctor So-and-so was seeing to it and that no further assistance was needed, Sarah would have been completely satisfied. As it was, she was flummoxed.

It was Vinetta who regained her composure first.

"You must be thinking of my sister's child. They were here for a few days and, yes, the baby did have a very bad cough. It was so bad that they cut short their visit and went home."

"Are there any other children in the house?" asked Sarah, her professional interest aroused. "Whooping cough is an infectious disease, you know."

"No other children," said Vinetta. "And I don't know that it *was* whooping cough anyway. We just thought it might be. They will be checking with their own doctor, I've no doubt. Now, if you will excuse me, I'll have to go. The telephone's ringing."

With those words, she shut the door.

"She was lying," said Anthea. "I am sure she was lying. There are children there all the time. And teenagers. I've seen them. Why should she want to tell you lies?"

Sarah Benson had had years of experience visiting people in all sorts of places.

"It doesn't matter," she said. "The house looks above reproach. The woman sounds competent. Even if she is

104

telling lies, that's her prerogative. She saw me as an un-
wanted intruder and she turned me away. And, if you
think about it, I had very little right to go there in the
first place.''

Connie agreed. Anthea gave the two older women a
look of irritation. They were much too easily satisfied.
People, she thought, should not get away with telling lies.
People, she thought, never did tell lies unless they had
something to hide.

After Sarah left, Anthea went to the upstairs sitting-
room and sat at the window gazing across at Number 5,
the house of mystery.

It was three o'clock in the afternoon. No one was coming or going at any house in the street. Anthea's thoughts
prowled round looking for prey. Then came inspiration.
Meet fire with fire, lies with lies. She picked up the
telephone.

''Hello,'' she said. ''Is that Mr. Mennym?''

''Sir Magnus Mennym speaking,'' said the voice at the
other end of the line. ''Is it my son you wish to speak to?''

The voice was overbearing, ponderous, intimidating.

Anthea cleared her throat and said, ''This is Castledean
Education Department. I am Miss Brown. We are conduct-
ing a survey to assess the need for school places in the
town over the next ten years. Could you please give me
details of all children in the house of, or under, school age
and which educational establishment, if any, they are . . .''

Sir Magnus interrupted.

''No,'' he said. Very loudly. And he slammed down
the receiver.

Anthea looked appalled. Connie, who had come into the

room in the middle of all this, also looked appalled, but not for the same reason.

"Anthea Fryer! How can you stoop so low! You dare to criticize other people for telling lies! And don't pretend to be genuinely concerned. We've lived here for five years and in all that time we hardly noticed the neighbors till last year's crisis. What they do or don't do is none of our business. You could get yourself into serious trouble pretending to be a council official. It's against the law, apart from any other consideration."

Anthea looked at Connie's stern face and felt both ashamed and embarrassed. Feet first again! She bit her lip. Part of her was still stuck in the Fourth Form, and Connie bore a fair resemblance to Miss Fenwick of whom one went in fear and trembling.

"I didn't think," she said. "It seemed a good idea. I just didn't think. Oh, Connie, why do I do such stupid things?"

Connie sighed, but in a friendly way.

"You'll grow up some day," she said.

"I *am* grown up," said Anthea, angry with herself. "I'm as grown up as I will ever be!"

"Of course you're not," said Connie. "Maturity takes a long time. I once read somewhere that the Ancient Greeks went to school till they were thirty-five."

Anthea smiled.

"Now," said Connie, "from this moment on, you just think about your own life. There's the wedding to prepare for. And we'll all be moving before the year's out. Let's forget all about the Mennyms. They are no concern of ours."

But the residents of Number 5 did not know how trivial the threat to their safety had really been. As far as they were concerned, officialdom had become interested in them. They believed, more than ever they believed, that the alien outside world was about to invade.

✥19✥

Back to Square One

Joshua was on his way to work that Friday evening when he saw the notice pinned on the inside of the front door. In the most ornate of copperplates, surrounded by a border of twirls and flourishes, it read:

> *NO ONE IS TO LEAVE THIS HOUSE*
> *TILL FURTHER NOTICE.*
> *THIS DOOR MUST REMAIN CLOSED.*

There was no signature, but the style and the hand were sufficient in themselves to identify the writer.

Joshua read it, took a deep breath. And opened the door anyway.

That can't refer to me, he decided. I *have* to go out. How else would I go to work?

At that time in the evening, no other member of the household had any thought of going out. When, some hours later, Soobie took his late-night jog, he did not see the interdict. The lobby was dark, and that was as it had to be for the house door to open and close without the risk of his departure being observed.

Tulip, of course, knew all about the notice. Under orders from Magnus, it was she who had pinned it there.

Vinetta first saw it next morning as she checked to see if the postman had been. Every nuance of its meaning was quite clear to her. Tulip must have told Magnus of the health visitor's interest in the family, and he was signaling panic-stations. Perhaps, she thought uneasily, this time he could be right. Vinetta did not know anything about the telephone call from the Education Department.

"So what happens next?" she asked Tulip, guessing that the notice was simply an opening flourish. "I see Magnus is putting up the barricades again."

Tulip was barely speaking to Vinetta by this time. She, of course, knew all about the phone call Magnus had taken, and she had guessed that her daughter-in-law was holding something back over that whooping cough business. There had to be a connection.

It was seven-thirty in the morning. Very soon Joshua would be returning home from work. Tulip already knew that he had ignored the notice pinned to the door. Another reason to be disgruntled!

She gave Vinetta a very prim look before replying.

"There is to be a meeting this evening," she said. "Everyone is to attend. It is vitally important."

So once again Joshua's Saturday at home was ruined. The whole family were summoned to take their places in Granpa's room at seven o'clock precisely. They sat themselves down on chairs and cushions, then watched in wary silence the angry old man sitting bolt upright in his bed. The purple foot was stretched out stiff and rigid. Uneasy minutes were spent waiting for Sir Magnus to give utterance as if he were some ancient oracle.

Tulip sat in the armchair looking round very severely. She had not even brought her knitting to this meeting.

Joshua, in his chair by the door, was hoping that it would all be over soon, whatever it was. He kept his counsel, but he secretly believed that his father was too apt to create irritating mountains out of molehills. Vinetta and Hortensia, seated side by side, both felt uneasy, knowing that they shared a secret. Pilbeam and Appleby were also uncomfortably aware of something untold. Soobie, innocent but acutely conscious of all the undercurrents, waited for the storm to break.

When Magnus finally spoke it was in a surprisingly quiet voice, but chill as iced water.

"A house divided against itself cannot stand," he began. "It is sure to fall. There are serpents in our midst. We are in the gravest of dangers and someone in this room knows how it has come about. Someone in this room has betrayed us to the enemy."

Miss Quigley looked terrified, Vinetta anxious. Pilbeam glanced guiltily at Appleby, who shrugged one shoulder and raised a defiant eyebrow.

Wimpey, puzzled by it all, was about to speak when Poopie gripped her arm in warning. They were twins after all. They might squabble and bicker day in, day out, but he was not going to allow her to step into the lion's mouth.

Just as well.

Her grandfather's next words came out in an angry roar.

"I want the truth," he said, "and I want it now. Which of you has had truck with the world out there? Which of you has caused this house to come under scrutiny? Speak up. Let me know the whole of the damage. I am the one who will have to repair it."

He collapsed back on his pillows.

Tulip, quiet, firm, businesslike, told them about the telephone call from the Education Department, and then, looking at Vinetta, said, "I think we should start with you. There is a story behind the whooping cough. It needs telling, whatever it is you are hiding."

Vinetta was about to speak when Miss Quigley gallantly interrupted.

"There is a story," she said, "but it is my responsibility. So I am the one who must tell it."

Bravely and with no fluttering at all, Hortensia told what had happened as she returned from the park.

Vinetta gave her a look of deep approval.

Tulip said scornfully, "So much for your vaunted ability to deflect attention. Magnus was right. He has been right all along. To take a big, old-fashioned perambulator out into the street was inviting trouble. It is only surprising that it did not happen sooner."

Pilbeam, seeing Miss Quigley look upset, and feeling respect for her courage, decided to take some of the fire.

"I think we should tell them all about our visit to *Sounds Easy*," she said, looking at Appleby. "We were spotted there, remember. Miss Quigley is not the only one to blame, if blame is the right word.''

Appleby looked frantic. For a split second she thought that Pilbeam intended telling them about Tony and the letters and her visit to the disco. Pilbeam, realizing what was going through her sister's mind, quickly told the simplified version. Never would she betray the confidence Appleby had placed in her. Their friendship was too precious.

After Pilbeam finished speaking, Magnus made his considered pronouncement.

"We must go back to square one," he said with his usual flair for finding the *mot juste*. "And this time not even Miss Quigley can go out. Till we are satisfied that it is safe to do so, no one must leave the house.''

Joshua had sat silent, but now was his time to speak. In a voice that brooked no contradiction, he said, "That won't do. No matter what you say, Father, I shall be going to work as usual tomorrow night.''

Soobie approached the problem less stiffly, but with the same end in view.

"I never go out before dark," he said, "even if it means waiting till nearly midnight. No one sees me. We cannot break all contact with the outside world, Grandfather, however much you might want us to. Letters need to be posted, bills have to be paid . . .''

"I do that," said Appleby sharply.

"Not anymore," said her grandfather. "You are one who must stay indoors. But Soobie has a point. And letters can be posted at any time of night or day. Soobie can post them.''

Appleby was furious.

"What about stamps?" she said. "What about envelopes? Soobie can't go to the shops."

Magnus gave her a triumphant look.

"Why do you think I have been buying so many these past weeks? A very elementary precaution. I have a supply of stamps and stationery which could last us six months, maybe even a year."

"You can't put parcels in a letter-box," said Appleby, looking at Tulip.

"No parcels," Granpa conceded. "Harrods will have to wait for their next consignment. Your grandmother will have to write and tell them she is unable to take any more orders just now. That's all she need say."

"Matches," said Appleby. "What about matches?"

"We have laid in enough of them to build St. Paul's," said Magnus with relish, "and Westminster Abbey too, if need be."

That sounded odd, thought Poopie, but very interesting. He looked at the grown-up faces and tried to follow the grown-up arguments. It suddenly occurred to him that his own life might somehow be affected. The garden, for instance. What about the garden? That was outside.

"But we'll still be able to do the garden," he said. "Won't we?"

"The back garden, maybe," said his grandfather, "but not the front."

"It'll grow wild," said Poopie. "Everything will just shoot up if it's not looked after."

Wimpey had a vision of plants climbing high to the sky and hedges meeting across the front path.

"It'll be like in the fairytale," she said. "We could be trapped for a hundred years. And Albert Pond might have to come and chop it all down."

Sir Magnus frowned at the mention of Albert's name, but as he looked at his little granddaughter he softened.

"It won't be a hundred years," he said gently. "A few months should be enough."

❧ 20 ❧

Some Birthday!

A birthday's not a birthday without any presents . . .

On the eve of the fourth of July, the day on which Appleby always celebrated her fifteenth birthday, Vinetta had gently explained that there would be no gifts to unwrap this year. No one had been to the shops.

"You could have bought things mail order," said Appleby. "It was the one thing I was looking forward to. If you'd wanted anything for *yourself* you'd have got it mail order. Why don't you just tell the truth? You all forgot. You were so busy worrying about what the neighbors would think or say or do, you forgot all about my birthday."

A six-year-old Appleby was inside her somewhere, desperately disappointed that there weren't going to be any birthday presents.

"We can still have a party, with the table set as usual," Vinetta said, trying to improve things but not succeeding.

"You must be joking," said Appleby. "If you lot want to have a party, you can have one without me!"

"Well, later then, when the siege is over . . ."

"Forget it!" said Appleby. "Just forget it. That's something you shouldn't find hard."

The expression on her face was ugly, the tone of her voice distressingly rude.

But Vinetta appreciated how disappointed her volatile daughter was feeling and she merely said, "Very well. We'll talk about it some other time."

The past few weeks had been very fraught. To go no further than the back garden, to have someone constantly on watch at the front window, was wearing on the nerves. There was a rota for guard-watch. Soobie's seat by the window made him the obvious choice for the job, but he wanted time to read, or even to go to his room and listen to the radio. Looking out of the window voluntarily was one thing, deliberately and carefully watching every minute of the day was quite another. So they took it in turns.

In those weeks they saw people coming and going at all of the houses in the street, but infrequently. There were long spells when the street was completely empty. On one occasion there was a flutter of panic when Anthea stopped to speak to old Mrs. Jarman just outside the front gate of Number 5. Wimpey, whose turn it was to watch, tugged at Soobie's sleeve to make him look up from his book.

"Look, Soobie, look. She's there. That woman."

Anthea at that very moment was looking toward the house. They both saw her. She had her head turned in their direction almost as if she were pointing.

"She's looking this way."

But the panic was soon over. Mrs. Jarman had shrugged her shoulders and walked on and into her own drive. The two Mennyms saw Anthea staring after her, looking somehow put out.

"Well, whatever she said," said Soobie, "our next-door-neighbor gave her a very cool reception."

Wimpey had told all the others about it. Even she knew that it was not much of an incident, but it was a bit more exciting than watching the grass grow. Which it did! Whenever it was Poopie's turn to be on watch the sight of the overgrown lawn with its invasive dandelions grieved his gardener's heart. "Maybe it was our garden she was talking about," he said. "It must be the worst-kept garden in the street."

When Appleby went to bed on the eve of her birthday she was still fuming and beginning to direct her thoughts toward revenge. And the best revenge she could think of was a bid for freedom.

An hour after midnight, she crept out of her room, wearing her outdoor clothes, her tartan jeans and her old yellow anorak. She was in her stockinged feet, carrying her strongest shoes. In her shoulder bag she had all the money she had accumulated over the past unspending weeks. The younger members of the family had all been given pocket-money as usual with the idea that they might appreciate how money could grow if one was not constantly spending it. Vinetta, every bit as naive as Wimpey in some respects, had been responsible for this arrangement.

"After all," she had said, "the siege will end some time. They will enjoy having some extra spending money when it does."

Appleby knew just what to do with *her* extra money. It was an essential part of the escape plan. There was one important commodity she would definitely need to buy.

She walked swiftly past Granpa's room. There was a low light on each landing and in the hall downstairs. The house was never in total darkness. Appleby watched carefully for any movement as she tiptoed down the two flights of stairs to the ground floor. She held her breath when she saw a thin strip of light under the breakfast-room door. Granny Tulip must be working late. Why couldn't she sleep at night like everybody else! Appleby took extra care as she turned the brass knob on the door to the kitchen. It opened silently on well-oiled hinges.

Once in the kitchen, she had one more task before she could leave the house. She reached up to the shelf where the old tea jar was kept and removed the key to the shed. Then she put on her shoes and went outside. She had a torch in her pocket but she dared not use it yet. She stumbled across the dark garden to the wooden shed that stood near the back fence. Fumbling guiltily, she opened the padlock. Inside, the shed was quite spacious, as garden sheds go. To the left of the door were neatly stored and stacked garden tools and do-it-yourself equipment. To the right, under the window, was a long plank workbench beyond which, straddling the side wall, was some sort of monster covered with tarpaulin. This was the object of

Appleby's quest. Taking the torch from her anorak pocket, and pointing the beam well away from the window, she made her way past the workbench. The tarpaulin was pulled back to reveal ...

Albert Pond's scooter!

It had been in the shed ever since Appleby had lodged it there following her flight from Comus House. This was the country home Albert Pond had provided for the Mennyms when it seemed that the authorities were bent upon demolishing Brocklehurst Grove. The family had not been able to settle there. It was too isolated. Appleby had rebelled and had made her escape on the old scooter that had belonged to Albert's father. Having used it once, she could use it again.

Everybody knew, of course, that the scooter was in the shed, but over the months it had been forgotten. Joshua had placed the tarpaulin over it after one of those what-shall-we-do-about-it sessions that had ended in deadlock.

"If Albert wants it," said Joshua, "he knows where it is."

They all knew instinctively that Albert never would come and claim his property. At first, it had saddened Soobie to think of it. Poopie was tempted to sneak a look under the tarpaulin. But in a surprisingly short time the scooter was forgotten. Except by Appleby. Appleby never forgot anything that she might be able to turn to good use some day.

She folded the cover away and carefully wheeled the bike out into the open. It was not easy. The machine was heavy, much easier to ride than to push, but she would have to be well clear of the house before she would dare to start up its engine. The helmet, with the gloves inside, was still hooked on to the handlebars where she had left it.

What made her task even more difficult was that she dared not risk using her torch. She had to maneuver the vehicle very gingerly over the dark grass. She pushed it across to the flowerbeds at the side of the house, trying to get out of sight of the back windows as quickly as she could. Then after struggling through a patch of uneven soil, she got the heavy, cumbersome beast onto the welcome smoothness of the front drive. The worst part was over.

Wheeling the bike cautiously toward the gate, glancing back over her shoulder to make sure that the front of the house was in darkness, Appleby felt a sudden tingle of joy. The excitement was beginning and the torture of being confined to the house was nearly over.

Then suddenly, ahead of her, the front gate swung open.

"Where on earth do you think *you're* going?"

It was Soobie. A fine summer night. A long late run. He had jogged up the High Street and then down to the river. He had crossed the elegant Dean Bridge and returned by way of the sturdy Victoria whose strong pillars carried a road and a railway. Then up past the Market and back onto the High Street again. He felt tired but content, and almost unblue. The last thing he expected was to walk headlong into a crisis.

21

Questions and Answers

The scooter fell noisily onto the drive. Appleby glared at Soobie.

"You gave me the fright of my life there," she said angrily whilst her imagination ranged over the possible explanations she might be able to offer for being in that place at that time with *that scooter!* A quick look up at the house made her aware of a light going on at a first floor window. Poopie's room. It was going to get harder, not easier!

Soobie righted the bike and looked grimly at his sister, still waiting for the answer to his question.

"Well?" he said.

Appleby tossed her head.

"Not that it's any of your business, Soobie Mennym," she said, "but I decided that this bike was too much of a temptation. I was taking it out to dump it. Any one of us might have decided to go off with it somewhere. Even you."

"I need to know more than that," said Soobie, "a lot more than that. Dump it? Where? How?"

Appleby's thoughts flicked through all the dumping possibilities and drew out, like a card from a file, what she hoped would be a credible answer.

"I was going to wheel it down to the river and tip it over the quayside."

Soobie went shades bluer in the light that shone in on them from the street lamp.

"You vandal!" he said. "How could you even think of . . ."

He stopped himself in mid-sentence as he realized that he was being unutterably gullible.

"Come on, Appleby. The truth's what I want," he said, "and that isn't it!"

Appleby looked sulky. From the back of the house at that moment, dressed in her long velvet dressing gown and carrying a cricket bat, came Pilbeam.

"What's going on here?" she said. "I saw movement in the back garden. When I opened the window I heard scuffling. I thought we had burglars."

"It's just Appleby," said Soobie. "You won't need your truncheon! She was sneaking off somewhere with the bike. If I hadn't caught her, goodness knows where she'd have been heading by now."

Pilbeam looked at her brother and sister and the scooter propped up between them. They both seemed ready to stand there and argue all night.

"It's no use talking out here," said Pilbeam. "Let's put the bike back in the shed and go into the kitchen."

Before anything could be done, the front door opened just far enough to let a small boy squeeze through and draw it shut behind him. Down the drive came Poopie, dressed in his striped pajamas and with his hair unkempt from sleep. When he saw the scooter, he whistled.

"Who brought that out here?" he said.

"Me," said Appleby. "Do you want to make something of it?"

By now Appleby was thoroughly angry, as if everyone else were in the wrong, but she dared not vent her anger on Pilbeam or Soobie. Poopie was a softer target. His rages were juvenile and did not impress her at all. But he glared at her all the same and came back with an answer.

"Granpa will kill you when he finds out," he said. "I'd hate to be *you* when Granpa finds out."

"Hush!" said Pilbeam. "No one is going to find out. We will keep it a secret. Now let's get the bike put away and we'll go indoors to talk about it."

Soobie wheeled the scooter back to the shed. They covered it with the tarpaulin again and locked up.

"I'll take the key," said Poopie, with the proprietary rights of a gardener. "I'll put it away."

He ran ahead of them into the kitchen, climbed on a chair and put the key back in its jar. Then they all sat round the kitchen table and looked expectantly at Appleby.

"Now," said Pilbeam, "what were you hoping to do? Where were you meaning to go?"

Appleby's mind was rapidly searching for a plausible story but, as she looked at Pilbeam she realized, not for the first time, that her sister was not in the market for lies. Since the disco business she had been more suspicious than ever. No matter how expert a lie might be, Pilbeam wouldn't buy it. The next best thing was to come at the truth sideways.

"I'm fed up with being buried alive," said Appleby. "We go nowhere. We do nothing. We might as well not exist."

"So where were you going with the motor scooter?" Pilbeam insisted.

Appleby kicked her foot against the leg of the table making two plates and a jug rattle.

"Enough of that," said Pilbeam.

Soobie looked angry but stayed silent.

Poopie looked virtuous, but dared not speak. He loved Pilbeam. They all loved Pilbeam, but she could be almost as intimidating as Granpa.

Appleby looked from one to another, then spoke grudgingly.

"If you must know," she said, "I intended to return the scooter to its rightful owner."

Soobie gave her a sharp glance. That was the truth. It smelled like the truth. But how had she planned to do it?

"How?" he said.

Having come clean, Appleby began to regain her wits and her composure. It had been a good plan. She felt quite proud of it.

"I'd have taken the scooter back to Comus House. I'd have followed the same route as I did when I brought it here in the first place. Going back would be no harder than coming here. In fact, now I know the way, it would be easier."

"Comus House would be empty. What would be the point of going there?" asked Pilbeam. "It would be all locked up."

"I know that," said Appleby. "I'm not stupid. I'd have

climbed in through the library window. Then in the morning I'd have gone down the road to the nearest phone box and rung Albert in Durham. I'd have explained where I was and why. He'd have collected me and brought me home and sorted out Anthea Fryer as he did the last time. I could have had an exciting birthday and have solved the whole family's problems at the same time. And you have spoiled it all."

Soobie, older, wiser and much more sensitive than his sister, gave a sigh before speaking.

"Impossible," he said. "Impossible for all sorts of reasons. We must never contact Albert Pond again. You should have realized that."

"Just because Granpa doesn't like him . . ." began Appleby.

"It's not only Granpa," said Soobie. "Do you understand nothing? Have you no finer feelings, no sense of what is proper?"

Appleby was so far from having finer feelings that she did not even know what he was talking about. There might have been an argument, but the kitchen door opened. They all jumped to hear Tulip's voice say, "What are you all doing here at this time of night?"

Appleby recovered first and said, "We're having a midnight feast. We're celebrating my birthday. After all, nobody's bought me any presents."

She picked up one of the plates and thrust it at Pilbeam.

"Have a jam doughnut," she said.

Pilbeam lifted an imaginary cake from the plate and took a bite of it. Whatever she might think of pretends, she was certainly not going to give the game away to her grandmother.

Tulip looked at them suspiciously.

"Midnight feast!" she said. "It's well past midnight now. Get yourselves off to bed."

✥22✥

A Vintage Motor Scooter

It was Pilbeam's turn to be look-out. She moved her high-backed chair into the center of the bay window. To her right, in his armchair, sat Soobie doing an old *Guardian* crossword puzzle that had somehow escaped everyone's notice. Newspapers from Granpa's room usually filtered round the house before the dustbin claimed them. But for the past weeks there had been no newspapers at all. An unblemished crossword was a real find.

"I think we should do something about the scooter," said Pilbeam, keeping her gaze firmly on the street. It was two weeks since they had caught Appleby attempting to abscond.

Soobie looked up from the newspaper.

"I've thought about that myself," he said. "We can't trust her. It'll only be a matter of time before she tries the same stunt again."

"We could hide the shed key."

"Hardly," said Soobie. "Dad and Poopie are always needing it—and, remember, Dad doesn't know about the latest escapade. The fewer who know, the better."

"All right, then," said Pilbeam. "What do you suggest?"

"I could do what she claimed to be doing when I caught her. I could take the scooter out somewhere late at night and dump it."

"That doesn't sound too safe," said Pilbeam. "It's not something you could carry in your pocket and throw into a litter bin."

Soobie was thinking. Pilbeam watched Mrs. England taking her old collie out for a walk. The dog stopped to sniff at their gatepost and was pulled away.

"I wouldn't want the bike to be destroyed or vandalized," said Soobie. "It's a beautiful vehicle and in wonderful condition for its age. It might even be worth something."

"We could hardly go out and sell it!" said Pilbeam.

"But we could try giving it away," said Soobie, ". . . anonymously, to some deserving cause."

It was an attractive idea, but it still posed the problem of how and where.

"I'd have to leave it where the right people would find it and I'd put a note in the saddlebag explaining that it was a gift."

"But which right people," said Pilbeam, "and where?"

Soobie saw in his mind's eye a whole map of Castledean. There was the Oxfam shop on Albion Street. But if it were left there in the middle of the night, anyone might take it. Some youngster might smash it up and kill himself or someone else. That was a risk Soobie would not take.

"St. Oswald's," he said at last. "I'll leave it in the passageway between the house and the church. Then I'll ring the doorbell and hurry away."

"Risky," said Pilbeam.

"Not really," said Soobie. "The passageway is dark and I can be out of sight around two corners before anyone comes to the door."

So that night, at twelve-thirty, Soobie went to the shed and wheeled out the scooter. He put on the gloves and the helmet and crammed his own goggles into his pocket for the return journey. He waited till he had left the Grove before he started up the engine. There was very little fuel left but that was an easy problem to solve. A few yards up the High Street was a Shell Station, one of the smaller ones, but still open all night for petrol. The shop door was closed and payment had to be made at a small window on the corner. Easy!

As Soobie came out onto the main road again, he was tempted. It would be his last ride on the scooter, and there was enough fuel to spare. So, very carefully, he rode to the Victoria Bridge, crossed it and then recrossed the river by the Low Bridge. The lights on the river looked lonely. The streets were almost dead. Few cars passed. A police car came along, going in the opposite direction. Soobie, seeing it, decided to take no more risks. He went back onto the High Street and rode down toward the church where he had once prayed for help when Appleby was lost. As he came to the first of the three churches, the one boarded-up and awaiting a verdict on its fate, he stopped the engine, jumped off the scooter and pushed it the rest of the way along a dimly-lit, deserted road.

He turned into the passageway between the church and the presbytery. After taking off the helmet and gloves, he pulled on the hood of his tracksuit and replaced his goggles. To reach the house door he had to go through a wooden gate into a little garden. Soobie planned to put the scooter just outside and to leave the gate wide open.

He rang the doorbell. Then—panic! For the youngest priest was on his way out to make an emergency sick visit. He had been about to open the door when the bell rang. Soobie ducked his head, turned and ran.

"Here!" shouted the priest. "What are you up to?"

But Soobie was well away. The puzzled young curate came out into the alley and saw the scooter. In a hurry to be on his way, he went back into the house and called, "Father Joseph, Father Joseph, there's something peculiar going on down here. Come and see."

It was not till the next morning that the priests found Soobie's note in the saddlebag.

This old scooter needs a good home. It is a gift to the parish of St. Oswald's, to be used or sold, whichever you think best.

"That's all very well," said Father Patrick, the oldest and most practical of the priests, "but we don't know our legal rights, nor do we know the rights of the giver. We could be accepting stolen property."

"I'd quite fancy riding it," said Father Leo. "It's almost an antique, but a real beauty. Imagine riding round the parish on that!"

The old priest raised his eyebrows.

"We must tell the police," he said, "and let them decide."

It was an unusual case and the local police, who had more important things to do, would much rather have turned a blind eye. Two of them had in fact seen the scooter the night before.

"Look at that," Mick Storey had said as they turned to go down Sandy Bank. "I haven't seen a bike like that for years."

"I've never seen one in my life," said his younger colleague.

"Pity we're not going in his direction," said Mick. "We could have stopped him and asked him about its history."

That was all. But they both remembered the driver. Stockily built, late teens, early twenties, dark tracksuit, trainers, helmet, big gloves.

The reporter on the *Castledean Gazette* called in at the police station next morning, looking for a story. But the criminals had had a quiet night. The scooter story was the best his friends in the force could manage. Human interest there, and local people. It would fill up a few paragraphs . . .

Just after one o'clock this morning, a mysterious rider left an old motor scooter outside the presbytery of St. Oswald's Church in Moor Street. Father Leo McDonald, curate at St. Oswald's, caught a glimpse of the driver before he ran away. He described him as a young man wearing a dark blue tracksuit with the hood pulled well down over his face, his eyes hidden behind large, dark goggles. He may have been wearing a stocking mask.

"He ran off as soon as I opened the door," said Father McDonald. "This morning we checked the scooter thoroughly and found a note in the saddlebag offering it as a gift to the church. But the strange way in which it was delivered makes us dubious about our right to keep it."

Two policemen, patroling in their panda car, saw the same scooter half an hour earlier. Their description of the youth agrees with that given by the priest.

In the absence of any number-plate on the vehicle, the police have decided to list it as a piece of lost property. If it is not claimed within the next six months, St. Oswald's will be the richer by one vintage motor scooter in perfect working order.

One other person had seen the scooter that night. Anthea Fryer was just drawing her bedroom curtains as Soobie pushed the bike out of the gate. Anthea was sleepy, but not too sleepy to ask herself what the Mennym boy was up to this time.

"I know they're an odd lot," she said to herself, "but nobody will listen to *me*. I always end up seeming to be completely in the wrong."

❧ 23 ❧

Reading the Gazette

When Soobie returned from ditching the scooter, Pilbeam was waiting for him.

"You've been a long time," she said. "I was getting worried. I thought something must've happened."

"Sorry," said Soobie. "I didn't realize you'd be waiting. I had a last ride on it for old times' sake. But things went quite smoothly. No real problems."

"*Quite* smoothly?" said Pilbeam, guessing that something must not have gone exactly according to plan.

Soobie told her about the young priest opening the door too soon.

"That's all," he said. "It's nothing to worry about."

Soobie might be cynical about pretends, but when it came to the ways of the world he was more naive than either of his sisters.

The next day the whole family was told that the scooter was gone.

"It seemed wrong to leave it to rust," said Soobie, sparing Appleby the truth, "and there is no way we could have returned it to Albert Pond. He's probably forgotten all about it."

No one ever went out to buy a newspaper these days. So the Mennyms never read the story in the *Castledean Gazette*. But there were those who did.

"There!" said Anthea to Connie, pointing to the report in the *Gazette*. "What did I tell you? There is something fishy about those Mennyms."

Connie read the story, but looked puzzled.

"I don't see the connection," she said.

"The youth on the scooter was that boy from Number 5 who goes out jogging at all hours."

Connie smiled.

"He won't be the only young man wearing a dark tracksuit. That description could fit any number of people."

"Ah!" said Anthea, "but I *saw* him. I saw him wheeling a bike of some sort out of the gate of Number 5 very late, the night before last—just about the right time. That's too much of a coincidence."

Connie read the report again, very carefully.

"It seems to me," she said, "that the boy in this story hasn't done anything wrong. The reverse if anything."

"So far as we know," said Anthea. "Those priests don't seem too sure—and the police obviously don't know what to make of it."

Connie gave Anthea a look of exasperation.

"What am I going to do with you?" she said. "It's none of our business. If your father weren't off to Scotland again, playing with his new house, I would really feel like having a word with him about your Mennym-fixation."

Anthea was indignant.

"I haven't got a Mennym-fixation, or any other sort, and I don't want to share Dad's psychiatrist, thank you."

"Listen to me then," said Connie. "Your mother will be home for good in September. You'll be married in October and off to Huddersfield. And in November the rest of us will be going to live in Scotland. Brocklehurst Grove will be a bit of the past and these mysterious Mennyms will be a memory. Don't get involved."

"Get involved?"

"I know you, Anthea Fryer. I should by now. You'll be off down to that police station making allegations and signing statements. There could be investigations and court cases with you as a witness. Your father would be annoyed and your mother would be embarrassed."

Anthea drew herself up haughtily.

"So what?" she said. "It's my life, isn't it, not theirs?"

"What about civil liberties?" said Connie, trying to get Anthea onto one of her safer hobby-horses. "The Mennyms have their rights, too."

"No one has the right to steal a motor scooter and give it away," said Anthea.

"You did see him pushing it out of his own drive," said Connie. "We don't know that he stole it."

"We can have a pretty good idea. He may even have stolen it from his parents. It is a vintage model, by all accounts."

"All right," said Connie. "His parents may have asked him to dispose of it for that matter. It may not be open, but it could still be perfectly above board. Let's change the subject. Bobby will be here in half-an-hour."

"Don't you dare mention this to him," said Anthea. "He's worse than you are."

"A good job, too!"

Anthea was on her best behavior for the next two days. But then, after a late night out, she came home, drew her curtains again, and saw Soobie jogging past her front gate.

He could be any sort of felon, thought Anthea. I have my public duty and I am being talked into neglecting it.

So early next morning, Anthea went out to the nearest telephone box and gave her information to the police. She did not tell them her own name and address. That way she could keep out of it. But she would watch for developments. She was sure there would be some.

Mick Storey glanced over the day's briefing sheet. The phone call about the scooter was low priority as far as the police were concerned, but Mick was interested.

"We'll be passing that way this morning," he said. "I think I'll call in and check it out."

"Waste of time," said his partner.

"Maybe," said Mick, "but I'd love to know more about that bike."

❧ 24 ❧

A Constable Calls

Poopie and Wimpey were in the back garden on the wooden chute. To be more accurate, Wimpey was playing on the chute and Poopie was having an occasional turn in between weeding the flower-beds. It was a day out of a fairytale, a jewel of a day, warm and sunny but fresh as a lily.

Joshua was resting on the sofa in the dining-room. The window was open, as were the windows in the kitchen and the breakfast-room. Pilbeam was helping her mother rearrange the top shelves. Granny Tulip was knitting a waistcoat, one of a batch she would be sending to Harrods when the siege was deemed to be over. In the day nursery, Miss Quigley was busily "bathing" Googles and looking forward to a few hours' painting in a sheltered corner of the garden. The back garden, of course. Nobody was allowed to work or play at the front of the house.

At 10:37 a.m. a police patrol car drew up at the front gate of Number 5 Brocklehurst Grove. Mrs. England, walking her dog, saw it arrive and wondered briefly and vaguely why it was there. Anthea, out shopping, missed it.

"I don't suppose I'll be long," said Mick as he got out

of the car. He stood a moment with one hand on the front gate and looked around. They could do with a gardener, he thought, observing the long grass and the generous scatter of weeds.

It was Soobie's turn on watch. His books and papers were laid aside and he was being attentive to the world outside the window. Seeing the policeman standing by the gate, Soobie sensed imminent disaster. Words might not be enough to keep this one at the door.

The gate opened. The policeman walked up the drive. Soobie dashed into the kitchen.

"The doorbell's going to ring, Mother, but whatever you do, DON'T ANSWER. Close that window. Close *all* of the windows. Everybody must be told to lie low."

Vinetta did not ask why. She hurried to the dining-room to warn Joshua. Pilbeam dashed upstairs to tell Appleby. Soobie went to the day nursery.

"Freeze," he said to Miss Quigley, who at that moment had Googles sitting in an empty bathtub and was pretending to squeeze water over her head from a dry sponge. "Just stay in here, but make no movement. If he looks in through the nets he will see nothing clearly, but he might detect any movement."

The doorbell rang.

But the twins, the young twins, were still in the back garden. Soobie heard Poopie's voice and ran to the back door.

"Come in, the two of you. Hurry in. Now."

"What for?" said Poopie.

"Never mind what for," said Soobie, diving out and grabbing them by the arm. They did not struggle, but rather took fright and needed no further encouragement to run indoors. They locked and bolted the back door behind them.

The doorbell rang again.

Nobody at home, thought Mick Storey, not surprising, lovely day for a trip out. He went round to the back and tried the back door, noted how much tidier than the front the back garden was. All secure, and no one in sight. Even the shed was padlocked.

"Nobody in," said Mick to his partner.

"So that's that."

"I might give them a ring tomorrow," said Mick. "If the bike's ownership can be established, I might be tempted to buy it. I'm sure St. Oswald's would rather have the money."

The younger policeman gave a grin of disbelief and drove on.

Soobie saw the car leave the Grove and called to his mother. "It's all right now. They're gone."

Granny Tulip came into the lounge and stood behind Soobie, her knitting still in her hands.

"I wonder what he wanted," she said. "It must have been something to do with that scooter. If you'd asked me, I'd have told you not to take such a risk. It was totally unnecessary. That bike was eating no meat in our shed."

Soobie winced at the acid in her voice. It was not the words. It was the way she said them. But she was right. What other reason could a policeman have for calling at 5 Brocklehurst Grove?

This was confirmed the very next day.

The phone rang.

Tulip picked up the receiver.

"Hello," she said. It was always her habit to wait for the caller to declare himself.

"Mrs. Mennym?"

"Lady Tulip Mennym speaking. Who are *you?* What do you want?"

The voice was sharp and deliberately off-putting.

Mick Storey said quickly, "This is Castledean Police Station. We've had a motor scooter handed in . . ."

Tulip interrupted.

"I do not see of what possible concern that can be to me. We do not possess a motor scooter. We have never possessed a motor scooter, or any other sort or variety of vehicle."

"Sorry to have troubled you," said Mick Storey, "but information led us to believe that the bike might have been stolen from your premises."

"Then I am afraid you have been misinformed."

"I'm sorry," said Mick again.

"No need to be," said Tulip. "Anyone can make a mistake."

Even Soobie, she thought, and felt very cross with that young man.

❧ 25 ❧

Then There Was One

The conference, the inevitable conference, that followed was the most tempestuous they had ever held. Even the overture was a clash of cymbals, not the quiet, sneaky introduction Sir Magnus usually employed when he had bitter things to say.

"Sit down, all of you," he barked, "and be quick about it. I have no patience left. This family is so utterly stupid that they go from one disaster to another. Talk about the slippery slope! You cannot blame the authorities this time. If the house comes down about our ears, you have only yourselves to blame."

They all sat looking miserable and awkward. Even Appleby was not her usual brash self. She had reason to feel uncomfortable about what might follow. Her own brief escapade with the scooter was still a secret. Pilbeam and Soobie had said nothing so far. Poopie was much better at keeping a secret than his twin. But would they weaken? Or, worse still, would they decide it was their duty to tell the whole sorry story? She had no worries about the disco affair. She had not been found out on that one, and she was not going to be found out. Time is a great concealer.

"You are all to blame," said Magnus. "All of you. If there is a single exception it could only be Appleby."

The others looked up in surprise.

"Appleby?" said Vinetta. "Not that I want to blame her, but I really can't see why she is more above reproach than the rest of us."

"Let me explain," said Magnus. "Let me go through the catalogue. You, daughter-in-law, have interfered at every turn, calling an end to a siege that most certainly had not ended, encouraging Miss Quigley to rebel. As for Miss Quigley, she let us down over the shopping and then she placed us all in jeopardy with that confounded pram. Go to the park! Feed the ducks! Idiot level."

He paused for breath and to give time to let his words sink in. Tulip eyed him, wondering what he would say of her. She didn't have long to wait.

"And you, Tulip, did not hold this family on tight enough a rein. I am bedridden, to all intents and purposes, I am bedridden. I expected my wife to give me constant and unwavering support. Did I get it? NO, I did not!"

Tulip drew in her lips in a pout of annoyance but said nothing. Let Magnus pass on to the others, the ones who were really responsible, her private quarrel could wait.

"Then we come to the younger generation. Pilbeam, gadding off to the theater and drawing attention to herself in all that frippery. And finally, Soobie, the only blue Mennym, the one face that could not pass in a crowd, goes for a ride on a scooter that does not belong to him, and is actually seen dumping it outside a church!"

At these words, Soobie was filled with a deep, defense-

139

less sorrow. I am as I am, his heart said. I have learned to accept what I am. Please leave me be.

Vinetta, too, was deeply wounded. Magnus knew how to hurt.

"At least," said Vinetta, "you can see no harm in Appleby. I suppose I must think myself lucky to have one daughter who meets with your approval."

Soobie looked at Appleby, was tempted to speak out but couldn't. She was his sister, and if she was totally treacherous with no real feeling for anyone but herself, that was something they must all accept. Soobie could not help being loyal. Loyalty kept him silent.

Pilbeam, knowing even more of Appleby's misdemeanors, looked across at her, willing her at least to acknowledge her own guilt about the motor scooter and to be generous in calling down blame upon herself. Not a hope! It was more than Appleby was capable of doing. She accepted her grandfather's verdict and had probably already forgotten every fault she'd ever had.

"Would that we could return to the old days when Appleby was my errand-girl," said Magnus, "the soul of discretion, the one I could trust completely! But that cannot be, not for many a long day yet."

Vinetta was about to remind Magnus of Appleby's many faults, but one look at her daughter made the words die on her lips. The red-headed, green-eyed Mennym was sitting on the rug with her feet tucked under her looking as comfortable and secretive as a cat. The humiliation would be too great.

"So what are we to do now?" said Vinetta. "You have blamed everyone but Appleby and Joshua, though no doubt you will find some harsh words for him before the evening's out. But come to the point, Magnus. We are here to consider what needs to be done, not to spend useless hours in recrimination.''

It had been a daylight meeting, not dark enough on the July evening for the curtains to be closed. But now clouds were gathering above Castledean and the sunset was turning from red to dull purple. Inside the room was a grayness both actual and spiritual.

Joshua rose from his seat by the door and switched on the light. Pilbeam, who was nearest, pulled the cord that drew the curtains. No one spoke. They just waited helplessly for Magnus to answer Vinetta's question. What were they to do now? How would this latest intrusion change their lives?

"The net begins to close," said Magnus. "We must all stay indoors. Even Soobie. For now any policeman seeing him out at night might feel called upon to stop and question him. Even the back garden will have to be out of bounds."

Joshua looked suddenly alert.

"You cannot stop me going to work, Father. At no time has anyone paid any attention to *me*."

"I don't know whether that's true or not," said Magnus wearily, "but I'll have to accept it. We still need someone to go to the post-box. Bills have to be paid."

"What about the telephone?" said Tulip. "We have had some unwelcome calls."

"That has been seen to," said Magnus. "I rang the company yesterday. We are now ex-directory. Only our solicitor will be given the new number. Our isolation is as complete as I can make it. Front door and back door will be kept locked night and day. No one but Joshua will need a key and he will have to lock up as he goes out and as he returns. Tulip will take charge of all the other keys.''

Sir Magnus had no feeling of interest in these proceedings. Being under siege was no longer exciting. It was downright miserable. Things had truly gone from bad to worse. The time when Miss Quigley was able to go out by day and Joshua and Soobie had been free to come and go by night seemed a luxury now. They had even managed when three had dropped to two. Now it was down to one solitary Mennym, traveling through the darkness. How long could that last? The Mennyms felt defeated.

❦ 26 ❦

Letters to Albert

My dearest, dearest Albert,

I have tried to forget you, but I can't. Appleby tells me I must put you out of my mind, but it is impossible. Please come and visit us once more. Let us read poetry together again. Let us pretend we are not from two different worlds . . .

The letter was unfinished and unsigned. Another unfinished letter lay beside it on Appleby's dressing-table.

Dear Albert,

For practical purposes, it is necessary that you return to Brocklehurst Grove. Our neighbor, Miss Fryer, has taken too great an interest in our affairs. We are now unable to go about our ordinary everyday life without fear of detection. We cannot even go to the Post Office. My husband is unable to send any but the slimmest of manuscripts to his publishers and I have had to refuse orders from Harrods.

I am especially sorry for my grandchildren. They were always used to going out and about. Now they go nowhere. The garden is neglected and growing wild. We do not know which way to turn. Please come and help us.

This letter too was unsigned. Underneath it was yet another epistolary effort . . .

Dear Albert,

Our life is becoming unbearable. We cannot go out of doors at all. I mean that more literally than you can imagine. For the past two weeks I have not even been allowed to go into the back garden. They keep the back door and the front door locked. Except for Father, who still goes to work, we are prisoners in our own home.

And it is all down to Anthea Fryer, the woman you called the Amazon who lives at Number 9 . . .

The letters appeared to be written in three different hands but they were all the work of one demented teenager.

Appleby was thrashing around for some way out of the cage she felt herself to be in. Write to Albert Pond. Get him to come and help. But whose summons would he heed, and whose ignore?

The letters were practice pieces. Appleby left them lying whilst she went to the lounge to sit at the round table with Pilbeam and do a jigsaw puzzle they'd dug out of Pilbeam's cupboard. Anything to relieve the monotony! It was a circular jigsaw showing a map of the heavens.

Vinetta went upstairs to see Magnus and to try to reason with him about the Draconian laws that now governed their lives. As she came onto the top landing, she felt a strong draught from somewhere. Vinetta went along the landing to investigate.

Appleby's door was ajar. Had she left her window open? Vinetta went into the room. She closed the window, and was about to leave when she noticed that the draught had whisked some papers onto the floor. Vinetta stooped and picked them up. She did not mean to pry but at the sight of the name "Albert" she felt she must read further. With alarm, she read all three letters. And wondered what she should do. Then she felt guilty at reading letters not intended for her eyes. She put them back on the dressing-table and went down to her own bedroom to sit alone and think.

What was she to do about the letters? Confront Appleby? Admit that she had read them? Warn her against doing anything stupid? There would be a terrible row. Vinetta hated rows. Then it came to her that there was no way Appleby could post a letter to Albert at this time.

And when the siege was over, she would not have the motive for doing so. Only one person needed to be warned at present. It was possible, more than possible, that *he* might post a letter without bothering to read the address on the envelope.

"Whatever you do," said Vinetta to Joshua, "don't post any letters for Appleby. I think she may have some idea of writing to Albert Pond."

When Appleby perfected the letter she wanted to send, however, she made no attempt to persuade her father to post it. She simply watched her chance and stole a set of keys from Tulip's cupboard. The letter, she decided, would be a plea from Pilbeam. She would take it out and post it in the early hours of the morning. It would not be easy. Stealth would be necessary and, as for timing, luck would come into it. The whole venture might have to be aborted many times if Tulip should happen to be on the prowl.

Appleby reckoned without one factor. There was one thing she did not know. Tulip, ever suspicious, was in the habit of checking the spare keys to make sure that none had gone astray.

The letter was ready in its envelope, stamped and addressed. The house was silent. Appleby had heard Granny Tulip's voice speaking to Granpa as she went into the room across the landing. Hours passed by and then Appleby adjudged it safe enough to creep downstairs and tiptoe to the front door. It looked like being first time lucky.

Then, just as she had the key to the lock, the breakfast-room door opened shooting a beam of stronger light into the dim hall.

Appleby jumped. Turning round she saw her grandmother standing there looking fierce and powerful, her crystal eyes glittering.

"Give me that," she said, snatching the letter from Appleby's hand.

Appleby was too startled to resist. Tulip peered at the envelope to read the address, then tore it open. Appleby looked horrified as her grandmother adjusted her spectacles and began to read the letter out loud in tones that echoed through the hall.

"I have never heard such utter rubbish," she said when she had finished. "What sort of pulp do you read, madam, in your quiet moments?"

"You had no business to read that," said Appleby, suddenly shot through with anger. "That's my letter, not yours."

"Your letter? Then why has it got Pilbeam's name on it? Just wait till your grandfather sees this!"

Vinetta was standing at the top of the stairs. Wimpey had come up behind her. Both had been disturbed by the voices.

"What's going on down there?" said Vinetta.

"Appleby's taken leave of her senses, that's what," said Tulip. Turning back to Appleby she said, "Give me that key. And go straight to bed. We'll talk about this in the morning."

Appleby flung the key across the floor.

"Take your rotten key," she said, "and you know what you can do with it!"

Brushing past her mother and her sister, she dashed up the stairs and then up the next flight to the floor above, but then she went straight past her own room and clattered up the uncarpeted stairs to the attic. She slammed the attic door behind her and barricaded it with the wicker chests that were still there. Then she sat in the rocking chair and sobbed.

❧ 27 ❧

In the Lounge

"You humiliated her," said Pilbeam.

"She deserved it," said Tulip.

"No one ever deserves to be humiliated, no matter what they've done," said Pilbeam vehemently.

Tulip was naturally very angry with her granddaughter, but it was quite clear that she was also proud of her own masterly way of foiling the attempted betrayal. She had told with relish the story of the night before—from the trap she had set for whoever had stolen the key to the scene that had ended in Appleby's mad dash up to the attic.

"And she can stay there as far as I am concerned," said Tulip. "She can stay there till she's threadbare."

It was ten o'clock in the morning. Another warm, sunny day. Joshua had looked in after his return from work, felt the charged atmosphere and fled to his room. Poopie and Wimpey were in the playroom, supposedly playing Scrabble but really listening attentively to the raised voices.

Soobie, in his chair by the window, was deep in gloom and had little to say. The others—Tulip, Vinetta and Pilbeam—made up for his silence. The events of the night before needed to be chewed over and over like cud.

"I read some papers I found in her room. They must have been practice letters," said Vinetta to Pilbeam. "I felt as if I shouldn't have done, but when I saw Albert Pond's name I couldn't help myself."

She told of the draught that had blown them to the floor at her feet. She looked uncomfortable as she waited for Pilbeam's reaction.

"You did nothing wrong, Mum," said Pilbeam. "You were sensible to warn Father against posting anything for Appleby. And you didn't embarrass her with any confrontation."

"And what I did was wrong," said Tulip. "Is that what you are saying?"

Tulip was bristling with anger.

Pilbeam said, "Yes, Granny, I think it was. But maybe you couldn't help it. You were under stress. We are all under stress."

She did not add that, to her way of thinking, only one person was to blame for all their miseries—the paranoid tyrant in the bed upstairs.

"How dare you make excuses for me? I am not senile!" said Tulip. "Why don't we just concentrate on the real culprit? Appleby was about to leave this house, using a stolen key, to post a forged letter to Albert Pond. Hardly the actions of an innocent! What would you have done if you'd caught her, Pilbeam know-it-all? Let her go?''

"No," said Pilbeam. "I would have made her give me the letter and the key.''

"As I did.''

"Then I would have read the name and address on the envelope. But I would not have opened it. I would have told her in no uncertain terms that writing to Albert Pond was not on. Then I'd have torn the letter, unopened, into little shreds.''

"You would never have known that she'd forged your name," said Tulip, "that she'd written stupid drivel and put *your name* to it.''

"And what I didn't know would not have hurt me.''

Soobie looked her way, knowing suddenly that his twin had been hurt perhaps more deeply than anyone would ever really know. Hurt, and humiliated.

Tulip had the letter in her hand.

"I haven't shown this to Granpa yet," she said. "When he sees it and hears how his precious Appleby has behaved, he will be livid. He will be outraged.''

Soobie spoke.

"You must not show him the letter. You must not tell him anything about it. One mischief is leading to another.''

Tulip turned on him.

"So it's you now! Are you daring to tell *me* what to do?''

"Yes," said Soobie. "I am.''

Vinetta had listened to them all intently. Now she gave her views, more than her views, her intractable decision.

"Give *me* the letter, Tulip," she said. "I have had

149

enough anguish to last a lifetime. That letter has to be torn up and forgotten.''

Tulip always felt diminished when her daughter-in-law spoke in that tone of voice. She became what she was, a little old woman, and not what she fancied herself to be—the presiding matriarch.

''Give me the letter,'' said Vinetta again.

Tulip resentfully handed it over.

Tiny pieces of paper fluttered into the basket near the hearth.

''Now,'' said Vinetta, ''we have a much more difficult problem to tackle. Appleby has shut herself in the attic. I tried to go in there this morning and she has the door jammed shut. She wouldn't even answer me when I called. How are we going to persuade her to come out?''

''Don't bother,'' said Soobie. ''Granny was wrong about the letter, but that doesn't make Appleby an angel. Leave her where she is for now. She'll get bored soon enough.''

Their voices had become so quiet that the twins in the playroom could be heard arguing.

''But I won. You know I won. You're just jealous because I know more words than you do.''

''You were cheating,'' said Poopie. ''I don't believe that ''poggle'' is a real word. You make them up as you go along. It's not worth playing with you.''

The argument was beginning to sound too heated. Vinetta went hastily to calm things down.

❦ 28 ❧

In the Attic

Appleby sat in the chair in the attic and rocked herself to sleep. Sleep is a wonderful place to go when life hurts too much. And Appleby, at times so insensitive, at times so vulnerable, was deeply hurt. To be found out and to be made to appear so foolish was terrible. To be mocked by her grandmother was a searing pain. The hurt went deeper than pride. It gouged out her self-respect. *She* knew the letter sounded feeble. She could have done without hearing it read aloud in Tulip's waspish voice. And Mother and Wimpey looking down at her over the banister as Granny poured scorn like poison . . . It wasn't fair. It wasn't fair!

When morning lit up the skylights, Appleby was sleeping sweetly, looking very young and very innocent. She was so exhausted that her first awareness of the new day came when Vinetta tapped at the attic door and tried to open it. The door rattled but the barrier held.

"Come on, Appleby," said her mother. "Don't be silly. Come out and face up to things. Get it over with."

Appleby was a little surprised at something in her mother's tone. It suggested complicity, a willingness to support her daughter without considering whether she merited support. But, no matter what, Appleby was not ready to face the music yet. So she said nothing and Vinetta gave up and went away.

The day dawdled. By the time the sun had traveled over the ridge of the roof and was pouring its light onto the attic floor, Appleby was wide-awake, angry with everybody, and bored.

She got up from the rocking chair and wandered around the room. It had not changed from the last time she had shut herself in there, the time she had hidden from Joshua after her return from Comus House. Books, chests, junk and dust . . . all of them of equal value to the trapped teenager. She had made for herself a prison within a prison. Albeit a fairly large prison. The attic was the width and the depth of the whole house, a massive, floored area under the roof vault. There was another door at the far side, so deep in shadow that it could easily be overlooked.

Appleby came to this door, idly, without purpose. It was a mirror image of the door at the other side of the room—one side shorter than the other, following the slope of the roof. That's odd, thought Appleby, there's no other staircase. This must be a cupboard. I wonder what's inside. Her right hand went out to grip the door handle.

"Don't!" said a voice, and Appleby did not know whether the voice was in her head or in the room. But the hand that was about to turn the doorknob stopped in its tracks.

"Don't open that door," said the voice more clearly.

Appleby spun round and looked across the room. There at the far end, seated on one of the wicker chests Appleby had used as a barrier, was Aunt Kate.

"Who on earth are you?" asked Appleby, too amazed to be frightened.

Kate looked, as always, solidly built and completely unghostly. Just so had she appeared to Albert Pond.

"I am Kate Penshaw," she said. Her voice was faint but firm. Appearing like this was breaking a rule that till now she had accepted as inviolable. *Well, what do they expect me to do?* Her mind threw out a challenge. *This is an emergency. How else am I to deal with it?*

Appleby stared at her, open-mouthed, utterly amazed.

"You're a ghost," she said in a voice that was clearly testing the truth of her own statement. "You don't look like a ghost," she added.

"I don't feel like one either," said Kate. But she was growing shadowy inside. This unlawful interview was sapping all her strength.

"What do you want?" Appleby asked, still unsure whether the woman was really a ghost after all. "You don't look like a burglar."

"I should think not," said Kate. "I've been some things in my time, but never a law-breaker, not till now."

Appleby took a few steps toward her. She was just as Albert Pond had described her. Her hair gray and wiry, her face firm and sensible, her whole appearance very solid and real.

"Don't come any closer," said Kate. "Before you go too far into what I am, remember what *you* are."

"Well, what do you want?" said Appleby. "You must want *something*." There was a sharp impatience in her voice, now that she was not afraid. No one was immune from Appleby's rudeness, not even the woman who made her.

"I've already told you what I want," said Kate. "I am breaking one of the fundamental rules of my existence to come and warn you not to open that door."

Appleby tossed her head. "Why not?" she demanded. "It's just a door and it's in our house. I'll open it if I want to."

"You'll regret it if you do," said Kate. "I daren't tell you more than that. I have said enough already. Just remember, I helped to make you. I care desperately what happens to you."

The love in Kate's voice echoed round the room.

Appleby faltered. She looked down at the door handle. When she looked up again the ghost had disappeared.

For some moments, Appleby stood there like Eve tempted by the apple. She looked at the forbidden door and experienced a turmoil of feelings. To be defiant was second nature, but at the same time, what a tremendous thing had happened! She, Appleby Mennym, whose claims to mystical knowledge had been laughed to scorn, had been privileged to see and hear a real, live ghost. Her right hand reached out to the door handle again but her left hand pulled it away. If Kate thought it important enough to appear, then maybe opening that door really was too dangerous a venture. Besides, the door must have always been there. It always would be there. She could open it some other day.

There was no question of going back to sit in the rocking chair again. She could not even think of staying in the attic till darkness came. A ghost is a ghost. The shadows of the evening can strike fear. An imaginary spirit in the ether of the dark attic would be more terrifying than the figure of Aunt Kate had been. Appleby dismantled the barrier and went downstairs.

"So you've decided to show yourself," said Granny Tulip as Appleby came into the lounge.

"Come in and sit down," said Vinetta quietly.

The only other person in the room was Pilbeam. Appleby, weighing up the situation, sensed that her mother and sister were on her side, if only she said the right thing at that moment. It was not an easy thing to say, and she could not manage to say it graciously.

"I'm sorry," she said and looked at all three of them defiantly. "I got bored. People do funny things when they get bored. I hate being locked in. You just don't know how much I hate it."

"We all hate it," said Pilbeam with an accusing look at her mother.

"I know," said Vinetta. "It's not easy. I'll talk to Granpa again. I'll see what we can do about it. Perhaps it won't be for much longer."

Tulip said nothing, but she was far from satisfied. Magnus had accused her of not keeping the family on tight enough a rein. If Vinetta had her way, there would be no rein at all.

Appleby did not mention the ghost in the attic. That was a bit of knowledge she did not want to share with anyone, not yet.

❦ 29 ❧

Poopie and Wimpey

Number 5 Brocklehurst Grove was right in the middle of the side of the square furthest away from the main road. The rest of the street stretched out to either side of it like two arms bent rigidly at the elbows. People living either side had no need to pass the Mennym house and few of them did.

Watching for trouble could be very tedious, but Wimpey dutifully took her turn, two full hours three times a week. That was a very long time for a child of her age to sit still doing nothing but look out of the window.

One afternoon, early in September, Wimpey was sitting in Soobie's armchair gazing at the empty street. She had been there alone for almost an hour. In that time, Mrs. England had passed twice, walking the dog. A boy on a bicycle had ridden past. A car had left the drive at Number 3 and headed away in the opposite direction. Nothing ever happens, thought Wimpey. The only little flutter of excitement came when Anthea Fryer approached from the left and Mrs. Jarman came out of the gate of Number 4 and turned to go and visit Wendy England at Number 6. They would meet outside the Mennyms' front gate, as they had done once before. They might stop and talk again and look toward the house. It would be trembly frightening, but it would be something to report!

But they didn't stop to speak. Mrs. Jarman and Miss Fryer had had little to say to each other since the day the older woman had put the younger one very firmly in her place. The nosy newcomer, who had lived in the street for only five years, if that, had tried to make insinuations about the Mennyms. In all the time they had been neighbors, Mrs. Jarman had never spoken directly to anyone in the Mennym household, was no more than vaguely aware of their existence, but they were harmless, they were rooted in the street, and when they came under attack Mrs. Jarman felt called upon to protect them.

"Good fences," she said in conclusion, "make good neighbors."

After all those years she was suddenly able to throw the words back at someone who clearly needed reminding of the right to privacy.

Vinetta came into the lounge and looked fondly at the ten-year-old, sitting so still and so obviously concentrating. Mother love is a sort of magic.

"Tired?" said Vinetta.

"Not yet," said Wimpey, determined not to give in. "I've still got another hour to go before Soobie takes over."

"Seen anything?"

"Just the usual," said Wimpey. "Nothing dangerous or exciting."

"But that's good enough," said Vinetta. "That's the

way we want it to be. The longer it's like that, the sooner the siege will be over.''

Vinetta drew up a chair and sat beside Wimpey. They went on watching together for some minutes in silence.

"It is lonely being a rag doll," said Wimpey quite out of the blue.

"I suppose it is," said Vinetta, "but human beings can be lonely too. Remember Albert."

"But they grow up and grow old and they die," said Wimpey, struggling with ideas she was too young to comprehend. "What happens to us?"

"I've often thought about that," said Vinetta. She was the sort of mother who never talked down to her children, who took their questions seriously and tried to give serious answers. "I think we are not so very different from the people out there. We are part of some wonderful game, and when the game is over God will carry us safely home in his pocket."

The reply was childlike, but not childish. It was a sort of metaphor for what Vinetta truly believed.

The Mennyms, in their own way, were a godly family. Wimpey always said her prayers at night, even the scary one—*Now I lay me down to sleep, I pray the Lord my soul to keep. If I should die before I wake, I pray the Lord my soul to take.*

It was all part of the pattern of living. Now, with the hours spent doing nothing but stare out of the window, Wimpey for the first time was trying to grasp at realities. The protection of pretends was growing thin.

"What does Dad believe in?" she asked.

Vinetta smiled.

"His family, his job and Port Vale," she said.

"And will God carry him home, too?"

"I should think so," said Vinetta. "It has to be a very big pocket!"

The boy on the bicycle rode past again. Mrs. England stood at her door and said good-bye to Mrs. Jarman.

Poopie never took a turn on watch these days. He could not bear to look at the garden growing more and more wild and untidy. For the past three weeks he had not left his room. But he was not sulking and he was not bored. He had turned the whole room into a tropical jungle in which green-clad soldiers fought with the men in brown. It was a harmless war in which combatants died repeatedly, without really dying at all. In many long years of fighting the only real casualty had been the evil Basil who had lost an arm, but still fought on.

In one corner of the room, the stool supported a high look-out tower occupied by the greens. The browns, led by Hector, had control of a swinging rope bridge, real treasure bought as a Christmas present years before.

Poopie had no scruples about moving even the heaviest of his furniture round the room. His bed was pushed into the corner near the window. On the bed, Chief of Operations, was Paddy Black, the rabbit. His pink eyes looked as nervous as ever, though he was just an ordinary cloth toy who had never so much as twitched a whisker since Vinetta first made him, no matter what Poopie might like to pretend.

In normal times, Paddy stayed in the hutch Joshua made for him, polished wood, splinter-free, with a door made of copper wire-mesh. The hutch was needed for the war-games. It was the perfect prison for captured browns. The greens, who were usually on the losing side because their leader was baleful Basil, had to be content with a shoe-box. So the hutch and the box were prisons within a prison within a prison. Except that for Poopie his room was not a prison. It was a jungle stretching over miles of territory. Thought, as the poet once said, is free.

✷30✷

Appleby and Pilbeam

On a dull day at the beginning of September, Appleby and Pilbeam made their way up the attic stairs. It was Appleby's idea. Pilbeam did not know what it was all about, but she respected the attic as a secret place where secrets could be shared.

"All right," she said as they closed the door behind them, "what's the mystery?"

She was worried in case Tony had come back on the scene. With Appleby, one was never quite sure. They had seen him a few times from the window in the long, tortured weeks of August. He had passed the house on several occasions, never suspecting that he was being observed from behind the heavy net curtains. The Appleby episode had taken its proper place in his memory, somewhere below last term's feud with the history master, and a long, long way below the fifty he had made in the match against St. Bee's.

"You haven't been doing anything silly, have you?" said Pilbeam as she settled herself into the rocking chair, leaving Appleby to the less exalted position on the foot-stool. In the attic, which she still thought of as *her* attic, Pilbeam was queen. In her romantic view of things, she had slept there under a spell for forty years till her twin Soobie found her, and her mother brought her to life. The truth that she would never know was sadder, but more wonderful. For forty years she had lain unfinished in a wicker chest and Vinetta had done much more than bring her to life, she had made her up out of scattered pieces, fitting her together with loving care.

Appleby switched on the light because the day was so dreary. The attic was minus the round table, but apart from that it was pretty much as it was after Soobie had tidied it long ago. Even the old white-painted doll's house was still in the corner. Wimpey had wanted to claim it but Vinetta had said it was too old and too frail to be played with. The packing-case filled with junk, and the two wicker chests which Appleby had used to barricade the door, were back in place, bounding the "inhabited" re-gion. The other half of the attic was bare and dusty.

"You haven't been in touch with Tony again?" said Pilbeam when Appleby failed to answer her first question.

"Nothing like that," said Appleby. "Do you think I'm a fool?"

"Well," said Pilbeam, "now you come to mention it . . ."

It was not the wisest of things to say to Appleby, but no one is wise all the time. Strangely, however, Appleby did not fly into a temper. She just pulled a face and sat silent for a few seconds. It was not the right time for a row. Appleby had something else in mind.

"There's another door over there, you know," she began, nodding toward the far wall.

"Yes," said Pilbeam. "I know. What about it?"

"Have you ever wondered what might be behind it?" asked Appleby innocently.

"I know what's behind it," said Pilbeam. "It's perfectly obvious what's behind it."

Appleby looked surprised.

"What do you mean?" she said.

"Well, I saw it ages and ages ago. It is obviously built into the house wall. If it led anywhere, it would have to lead to some outside staircase."

"But there isn't one," said Appleby.

"No," said Pilbeam, "there isn't one now. There was one at some time. It was removed and the doorway has been bricked up from the outside. If we opened that door now, just supposing it still does open, we would see a brick wall."

"Then why did Aunt Kate forbid me to open it?" said Appleby, startled into forgetting her original plan. "And how do you know all that?"

"Come off it, Appleby!" said Pilbeam. "You've never seen Aunt Kate. If you really had you'd have told me long before now. You couldn't have helped yourself."

"I don't tell you everything," said Appleby, raising her

voice. "I don't tell anybody everything. You didn't tell me about the door either. You're no better than I am."

Pilbeam looked at Appleby calmly.

"There was nothing to tell, Appleby. I spent a long time in this attic, looking round and getting to know every part of it. I saw the door from the inside. Months later, I saw the house from the outside and the signs of a fire-escape that had been removed and brickwork that had been added. It was, I suppose, mildly interesting, but not hot news. Now, if you had really seen Aunt Kate's ghost, that would have been something else."

"Well, I did see her," said Appleby with gusto, "and I've been dying to tell you but . . ."

Appleby looked cautiously at her older sister and wasn't quite sure how to finish the sentence.

"But what?" said Pilbeam, beginning, rightly, to suspect that Appleby was up to her tricks again. Appleby was fun. She was lovable. She was vulnerable. But she was completely untrustworthy. It was a fact of life that every Mennym knew.

"But what?" said Pilbeam again, more insistently.

Appleby coiled a lock of her long red hair round her right forefinger. Pilbeam had long recognized this as a sign of prevarication.

"Come on, Appleby," she said. "Don't try anything on with me. I'll always be one step ahead of you. You know I will."

"Clever clogs," said Appleby sharply.

"Well, if you think I'm just here to be insulted, I'm going."

Pilbeam got up from the rocking chair and gave her sister a very cold look.

"Wait," said Appleby, jumping to her feet. "Sit down. I'll tell you all about it."

"No lies," said Pilbeam firmly, "and no more cheek."

They both sat down again.

"I was going to try and persuade you to open the door without telling you anything," Appleby began with unusual frankness, "but you took me by surprise when you knew all about it. Only you don't."

"What do you mean?"

"You don't know the whole truth about the door. It was when I ran up here after Granny was so nasty about the letter."

"Yes," said Pilbeam grimly.

"I had locked myself in to punish everybody, but I was getting bored. I looked round, pretty much as you must have done. I found that door and I was just about to open it when a voice warned me not to."

"A voice?"

"Yes. And when I looked round it was Aunt Kate. She looked just the way Albert described her. I suppose that's why I wasn't terrified."

"Then what?"

"She said something terrible would happen if I opened the door, and then she left."

"Disappeared?"

"I didn't see her disappear. I turned my head for a second and when I looked back she was gone."

Pilbeam looked at Appleby searchingly.

"So what do you think?" said Appleby. "Would *you* try to open it? Just to see if she'll come and stop you?"

"I don't want to open it," said Pilbeam. "There's no reason to. And if Aunt Kate's ghost really did tell you not to, then obviously you shouldn't."

"You don't believe me," said Appleby crossly. "I'm telling you the absolute truth and you don't believe me. It's not fair."

"It doesn't matter what I believe," said Pilbeam. "I do know it's pretty dodgy to open a door that hasn't been disturbed for years and is obviously not meant to be opened. Maybe that's what Kate meant. If you open that door you might make the whole house collapse."

"You must be a right idiot if you believe that!" said Appleby scornfully.

"I would be a right idiot if I believed what you wanted me to believe."

"Which is?"

"That that door is governed by some supernatural force."

"It could be," insisted Appleby, "and Aunt Kate definitely came and told me not to open it. I don't know how to make you believe me. I don't always tell lies. I am not telling lies now. Why don't you believe me?"

Pilbeam tried hard to be kind. Appleby looked so distressed. It could all be an act. Appleby was such a good actress. Pilbeam was not completely sure what to believe.

"I think maybe you dreamed it," she said. "You'd been awake half the night. You'd been upset by Granny Tulip. You must have dozed off and had a nightmare. Dreams can seem very real, you know."

"But . . ." began Appleby again.

"We will leave it at that," Pilbeam interrupted in her firmest voice, "and I think that you should stay out of the attic. It makes your imagination run riot."

She got up from the rocking chair and walked out of the room. Appleby, as usual, followed her reluctantly.

❧ 31 ❧

The Forbidden Door

Appleby stayed out of the attic for over a week. She played records and read old magazines and talked to Pilbeam. They stayed, as they had to stay, trapped indoors. Tulip kept a careful watch on everything. Outside, the late summer weather was temptingly bright but unattainable. The keys to the house were locked in a drawer, and Tulip carried the key to that drawer always on her person. Even the telephones were never left untended. The phone in Granpa's room had always been impossible to use, since the old man never left his bed. Now, purely to protect the phone, Tulip began to lock the breakfast-room door whenever she went to any other part of the house. There was no possibility of anyone ringing the police, or the fire-brigade, or Albert Pond. It was hard to keep one step ahead of Appleby, thought her grandmother, but not impossible.

Vinetta's attempts to get Magnus and Tulip to change

their policy had proved unavailing. They were so sure that their ideas were right, and Vinetta, always the reasonable one, was never completely sure that they were wrong.

"If we were very cautious," she said, "it might actually be safer to go out than to stay indoors all the time. Anthea Fryer might begin to wonder where we all are. She might even come round to see."

"And if she does," said Granpa, "she will see nothing. We shall not answer the doorbell. Anthea Fryer has no right to come anywhere near us. No one has."

So it was necessary to go on watching the street. Even Appleby took her turn at the window. That was also a time of distressing inactivity. She did think about telling them there was a prowler in the garden, or that smoke was drifting round the corner from the back of the house. But she recognized such pretends as feeble and abandoned them. And the worst of it was the way Tulip looked at her. It was as if she had stuck a notice saying, "Danger, unexploded bomb" round her granddaughter's neck.

"Why are you looking at me like that, Granny?" she said when Tulip came and sat beside her in the lounge, not wishing to leave her alone too long. "Have I suddenly sprouted another head?"

"You know why I am looking at you," said Tulip. "I don't care how much they all take your side, you are an untrustworthy little madam. And I am looking at you and wondering just what mischief's brewing in that brain of yours. I haven't told Granpa about the letter. It would distress him too much. But don't think I'll ever forget about it. I forget nothing."

Appleby gave her grandmother a sly look.

"The devil finds work for idle hands to do," she said, quoting one of Granpa's pearls of wisdom. "If I do anything wrong, it will be all your fault, yours and Granpa's. Keeping us all in here day after day is just asking for trouble."

"As long as we know where we stand," said Tulip. "Your grandfather has very wisely decided that we should all stay indoors for the duration . . ."

"What duration?"

"For the time it takes to be sure that it is safe to go out again. You don't like it, I know, but you will just have to put up with it. And I will have my eye on you night and day. You can be as cheeky as you like, and as defiant as you like, but you are not leaving this house. I will see to that."

At last Appleby could endure it no longer. So, one evening, just after Joshua had gone to work and the front door had shut behind him, she slipped quietly out of the lounge and went slowly upstairs. She knew that Pilbeam was in the kitchen with Vinetta. No one else in the family had any idea of the secret of the attic. Tulip's guns were pointing in the wrong direction!

As Appleby passed by her own room she thought, I haven't made up my mind yet. I might not open the forbidden door. I might not even go into the attic. So it was that she drifted into danger, not intent upon disobedience, but rather just toying with the idea.

But she did go into the attic. She sat down on the rocking chair and looked across the room to the shadowy door on the far wall. What were the possibilities? The house, as Pilbeam had warned, might collapse. Unlikely, thought Appleby, very unlikely. Or something might come into the room and devour her. Improbable, she thought, highly improbable. Kate might reappear. Possible, and interesting. Appleby had decided that there was no need to fear Aunt Kate. She was indeed a most unghostly ghost.

But, Appleby mused, it was more than likely that she would see nothing except a wall of bricks. Perhaps she *had* imagined Kate. She had had Albert Pond's description to go on, combined with a strong desire to encounter the supernatural, and she had been very upset at the time and very tired. All in all, opening the dummy door was neither here nor there.

The attic grew darker but for a long time Appleby, seated in the rocking chair, could not be bothered to go to the landing and switch on the light. When at length she got up to do so, the spirit of mischief took over and, instead of going out of the door behind her, she, like another lady grown weary of imprisonment, "made three paces thro' the room"—more than three paces! A dozen strides swiftly taken, and then she had her hand on the doorknob. She paused, waiting. But Kate's voice did not come to her in the gloom, a weakened Kate no longer had the power to appear to her beloved but totally irresponsible child.

The brass knob turned in her hand almost of its own accord. She made no attempt either to open the door or to keep it closed. It moved. Very, very slowly, very, very slightly.

Through the narrow opening came a thin stream of liquid light, magical, milk-white, honey-sweet and fresh as Spring. It was enough to captivate, to make anyone want

to fling wide the door and enter. Almost anyone. Not
Appleby. Suddenly, for the first time in her existence, she
was visited by a sense of the consequences of her own
actions and was filled with terror. Desperately she put her
shoulder to the door and tried to close it, but a power was
there that she had not reckoned with. The door wanted
to open.

And the more it pitted its strength against hers, the more
of the wonderful light filtered into the room. It bathed
the bare floorboards making the wood look precious as
diamonds. And there was music too, like water-bells chim-
ing far away. Whatever this was, it was another world and
Appleby knew that it could destroy her own, no matter
how beautiful it might be.

"Help me, Kate Penshaw," she cried. "Please help me!"
The power behind the door was growing stronger.

"Aunt Kate," shouted Appleby. "Please, please, please
come and help!"

❦ 32 ❦

Statues

Vinetta was standing in the kitchen. The large earthenware bowl was cradled in her right arm, in her left hand
she held the long wooden spoon. She was making a cake
for Sunday tea. The imaginary mixture would be poured

into the cake tin and then it would be left in the oven for precisely one and a half hours. After that it would be turned out onto the cooling tray in the middle of the kitchen table. Tomorrow a cardboard model of a cake would be put onto the turntable and carefully iced and decorated. It was not something Vinetta did every weekend, but she had baked cakes more frequently recently. It was a way of compensating herself for being kept indoors.

Just as she was about to pour the mixture into the tin, lined with real grease-proof paper, time stood still. Vinetta froze where she stood and became a statue.

At that precise moment, there were statues all over the house.

Sir Magnus, sitting up in bed writing yet another account of the Battle of Edgehill, was stopped in midsentence.

In this, the first battle of the Civil War, the physician, William Harvey of Folkestone . . . The pen was still touching the paper, the old man was bent forward over his work, but totally immobilized. His purple foot trailed on the floor.

Lady Tulip was in the breakfast room, knitting. In, over through . . . but not off. The loop stayed on the needle. Only the ball of wool took on a life of its own and rolled away into a corner.

In the day nursery, Miss Quigley had just finished putting Googles into her nightdress. She was making a fuss of her, holding her high up in the air and saying, "Who's my best baby?" And there was Googles, everybody's best baby, hands outstretched, giggling excitedly, when everything froze. There in the middle of the nursery was the tableau of a nanny holding up in front of her a baby as stiff and as still as a doll.

Pilbeam was going upstairs to her room, having left Vinetta in the kitchen only seconds before. She had suddenly found herself wondering what Appleby was doing. After all they had been through, worrying about her sister came as naturally to Pilbeam as it did to Granny Tulip. So she set out to see where she was. And then time stood still. Pilbeam was no longer worried. She ceased to think, to move, even to breathe. One hand gripped the banister, one foot was on the top stair of the flight, the other on the stair below it. In that position, she remained.

Soobie was alone in the lounge where he had been watching a program on TV about Wainwright's coast-to-coast walk. I could do that, he thought, as the titles rolled up at the end. I could secretly walk the breadth of England and all I would need would be a mackintosh and a spare pair of trainers. Some day, when the siege is ended, I think I will.

He crossed the room and bent down to switch off the set. And at that moment life ceased. The blue rag doll was just returning to the vertical and not quite well enough balanced to freeze without falling. It swayed and tumbled over and landed clumsily on the floor in front of the fire. A little too close. The bars were glowing. In a very short time the doll's navy blue hair would begin to singe.

In his bedroom, Poopie was pretending to feed Paddy Black, holding out a piece of green plastic that passed well enough for lettuce. He was sitting on the floor in front of the hutch. The room was still full of dead and wounded soldiers. Poopie had decided to play a different

172

game, but first he had to put away his army. This was no easy task and feeding the rabbit was a delay before the start. Poopie was lying on his stomach, leaning toward the hutch, his legs sprawled out on the floor behind him. The lettuce was held between his thumb and forefinger. And there it stayed.

Wimpey was already in bed, propped up against her pillows, reading *Rivals of the Chalet School*. At the moment when time stood still, Wimpey was turning the page. . . . *Her black eyes were half-open and her cheeks were scarlet. A tearing, rusty sound* . . . Wimpey read no further. The page remained unturned. The doll in the bed looked sweet and lovable, almost like a real little girl.

Whoever next crossed the threshold of Number 5 Brocklehurst Grove would find it full of intriguing tableaux. What questions there would be to ask! What are these dolls? Where is the owner of the house? It has not been long deserted. The electricity still works. The telephone still rings. The gas fires still warm the rooms. Where are the human beings who control everything? Where on earth can they be? The newcomers would feel they had stumbled upon a suburban *Mary Celeste*.

Ah, but that was not the worst of it. What about Joshua?

He had reached Sydenham's and taken the keys from Max the short-sighted, simple-minded laborer—a good worker and a good son to his widowed mother, but one of nature's children. Joshua appreciated this and felt safe enough with him to spare a word or two.

"It's a warm night, old son," he said as he held the door for him to leave. "More like July than September."

He closed the door and went to the solitude of his office.

He removed the overcoat that he always wore to walk through the streets to work, no matter how warm the night and he went to hang it on its peg on the coat-stand. He was just reaching up to do so when time stood still. He froze in the act. What did he look like? The effigy of a middle-aged man, grizzled hair, stocky figure, wearing a blue shirt and navy trousers. Only an effigy, a very good likeness. Not the real thing.

In the morning, Charlie would come in and see the doll standing there. Charlie was always the first to arrive. He was an expatriate cockney who after years in the north still thought of London as home. What would he think when he saw Joshua who was not Joshua? Blimey! What would he *think?* And what would eventually happen to the doll? Thrown away with the rubbish? Claimed by one or other of the staff? They might even call in the newspapers, or the police. They would surely send to Brocklehurst Grove to make enquiries about their nightwatchman. . . .

In the lounge there was already a faint smell of burning. What a calamity it would be if Soobie burst into flames and the fire spread till the whole house was ablaze!

In the attic, the mystic light spilling into the room made the floor glow vibrantly. The battle with the door was all but over. Appleby was finished, failing in her attempt to put right the harm she had done.

Oh, Kate Penshaw, Kate Penshaw, you were meant to leave your house in order! This is no way to settle your affairs on Earth. This is an appalling mess.

❧ 33 ❧

A Battle for Life

The earthenware bowl fell crashing to the floor and broke into a hundred pieces. With all the strength that was left in her, the spirit of Kate possessed Vinetta, the power of instinct telling her what she must do. Vinetta ran out of the room and up the stairs calling, ''I'm coming, Appleby. I'm coming, my love. Hold fast. Hold on.''

She brushed past the doll on the staircase, the immobile Pilbeam. She hurtled on up to the top landing then along to the attic stairs. Her footsteps echoed through the silent house. And when she went in at the attic door, instinct told her to avert her eyes from the glowing light and join her strength to that of her daughter.

It was a battle, even with all the energy Kate's spirit could supply. The door fought back. It had been winning. It was not about to give in easily. The battle became more and more fierce. On one side was Vinetta's unyielding love for her family, a passion that would outlast all other. On the other were the powers of destruction.

The door pushed till it billowed. The light became savage. It gave up promising paradise and threatened instead hellfire. Vinetta held on, her shoulder thrusting at the opening, her left hand gripping the frame, her right foot wedged against the door. The gap closed . . . an inch, then it opened . . . an inch. The contest became a desperate wrestling match. Appleby, recovering a little, drawing strength from her mother's presence, stood by her and made yet another colossal effort, pushing again, harder and harder, with the palms of both hands spread flat on the door above Vinetta's head. The two dolls were filled with a mammoth determination to win. But it was as if some giant full of evil energy were flinging himself against the other side. The floor beneath their feet creaked and groaned.

Outside in the growing darkness, storm clouds gathered above the Grove. The elements rushed to join in the fight, unruly, noisy elements, roaring like an angry crowd. Sheet lightning lit up the statue of Matthew James Brocklehurst and thunder burst like shells all around him. It shook the house and rattled the attic windows.

The force behind the door grew stronger and stronger till the two rag dolls, even with the spirit of Kate helping them, felt their power draining away.

"Keep on pushing, Appleby. Harder, harder," cried Vinetta, her voice barely audible above the noise. "If it wins, we must all die." She spoke with deep conviction, even though she did not fully understand what she was saying.

The lightning spread over the sky again, its blueness adding to the eerie light within the attic. The thunder crashed, rocking the rafters with its noise.

Then there was a sudden pause, a lull in the storm, as if the contestants were drawing breath, and at that moment Vinetta called out loudly, in a voice that was not her own, "Deliver us from this evil. Strengthen us against disaster.

176

Forgive me. Please, forgive me. This will never, ever happen again.''

The silence that followed this prayer was as deafening as the thunder had been. Then, with a long, mournful sigh, the billowing door collapsed, its handle turned and a lock could be heard to click shut. It was just a door again, an ordinary door. It was closed and the attic was left in deepest darkness. Mother and daughter sank to the floor, exhausted and terrified. There was no reserve of strength left in them.

They sat like two shipwrecked mariners washed up on an unknown shore. They slept. And, for one of them, it was the sleep of death.

The storm died away in a shower of rain that left the air fresh and clean. The moment the battle ended, Kate's spirit was free to leave the attic, and thus did life return to the rest of the Mennyms.

In the big front bedroom, Granpa Mennym went on writing . . . *was given charge of the young princes*. He did not know that for the past half hour he had been in a state of suspended animation, a state that might have continued forever had it not been for the strength of love.

Tulip looked at the clock and was vaguely aware that it was later than she thought, half an hour later, and that was puzzling. She did not usually nod off. To have done so was irritating. She looked down at her knitting, still secure in her hands. The loop left the needle and the stitch was complete. She felt uneasily that something was not quite right as she went to pick up the ball of wool that had rolled away on the floor.

In the lounge, Soobie was bewildered to find himself lying awkwardly on the hearthrug. There was a smell of burning and with a yell he sprang up and began beating furiously at the back of his head from which smoke was rising. To his horror he saw sparks escape from under his hand.

"Help!" he shouted. "Somebody help me!"

Pilbeam on the staircase heard his cries, sprang into life and ran down to the lounge.

She saw black smoke rising from her brother's head. Soobie was about to burst into flames. Pilbeam grabbed a cover from the back of the settee, flung it over his head and held it there. Her own hands felt the heat coming through but she kept her grip. The longer those sparks are deprived of air, she thought anxiously, the sooner they will die. Soobie understood and put his hands up to help. After a few minutes, Pilbeam slowly and gently uncovered the back of Soobie's head. The sparks were gone. The smoke was dying away.

"It's just about stopped smoldering," said Pilbeam, concentrating on the damage to the back of her brother's head. Soobie was frightened. This was a terrible unknown.

Pilbeam, knowing exactly how he must be feeling, said, "It's all right. There's not really much damage. Your hair looks more ginger than blue on the crown now and there's a bare patch about the size of a postage stamp, but Mother will be able to put it right. You are very lucky it didn't flare up. It could have been much worse. How on earth did it happen?"

"I don't know," said Soobie, feeling less alarmed now that Pilbeam had everything under control, and becoming annoyed with himself. "I'm blowed if I do. One minute I was turning off the TV, the next I was lying on the floor in front of the fire and beginning to smolder."

"I suppose you could have fainted," said Pilbeam. "People do faint."

Soobie remembered that Miss Quigley had once fainted.

"I don't think I'm the fainting type," he said. "And I had nothing to faint for."

Soobie sank down onto the settee.

"I can't think *how* it happened," he said, and was even more perplexed when he looked up at the clock on the mantelpiece. The program had finished, he had switched off the set. The act of a few seconds seemed to have taken over half an hour.

"I *must* have fainted," he said. "There's no other explanation."

For Poopie and Wimpey the change from inanimate back to animate was less dramatic. Poopie fed his rabbit and Wimpey continued to read the harrowing tale of Joey Bettany's brush with death. And neither of them was aware that there had been a break in the action.

Miss Quigley gave Googles one last hug before carrying her up to the night nursery. A glance at her watch told her that baby's bedtime was half an hour later than usual. Thirty minutes is a short time to the normal run of people, including rag dolls, but to a strict nanny thirty minutes is thirty minutes. Miss Quigley was mystified to discover that she was not running precisely to time.

Dragging herself awake at last, Vinetta said to Appleby, "Let's go downstairs." She stood up and reached one hand down to raise her daughter. "We must see how things are."

Her tone was gentle and weary. She was not even sure what her words meant. How should things be?

Appleby did not answer.

"Appleby," said Vinetta sharply, alarmed at her daughter's failure to reply, or even to attempt to rise. But the doll that was Appleby was slouched against the door, limp and unmoving. Vinetta bent down to the floor and Appleby's whole body lurched to one side.

"Appleby," cried Vinetta, her voice rising octaves in terror. "Stop being silly. Get up now and come downstairs."

The doll on the floor never stirred.

Vinetta knelt beside her and felt the lack of warmth, the solidity of fibre that was no longer buoyed by breath.

Can this be death? Can *this* be death?

Vinetta grabbed Appleby by the shoulders and shook her, and was alarmed to feel dust in the cloth she held and an unnatural hardness.

"Appleby, Appleby, for God's sake wake up," she cried. "The door is shut. It can stay shut forever. There's no need to die. To *die?*"

Vinetta let go and sat down again on the floor beside her daughter. She who had made the best of many a bad situation was defeated by this one. But there is a limit to every feeling, even despair. Vinetta did not know how long she sat there, but suddenly she became light-headed and detached from reality. She got up, crossed to the attic door, the real attic door, and switched on the light. Then she went back to her daughter's side and dragged her across to the rocking chair. With an effort, she lifted the dead weight onto the seat.

"You'll be all right," she said. "You'll be all right. Rag dolls don't die. Not one of us has ever died. Pilbeam once sat like you in that chair. Don't be frightened, love. It will come right. You'll see."

But the green glass eyes were totally vacant. The stuffed head hung on one side as if the doll had been badly made. Pilbeam's eyes had been living even when her head was still lying in tissue paper. Pilbeam's arms had been supple, her torso buoyant. She had been in a pre-life state. Appleby's state was post-life, dead forever. This was the fact that Vinetta could not bring herself to believe. So she pretended that her child was sleeping. She kissed the lifeless cheek.

"I'll have to check on the others," she said. "We have been in grave danger, Appleby. But we will come through. Kate will look after us. Patience is everything."

Vinetta left the attic, shutting the door gently behind her. She went down the stairs, holding firmly onto the handrail for support. The shock she had suffered was so great that she needed somehow to contain it and make it manageable. Pretend, pretend, pretend, pretend. If reality is too painful to bear, shut it out. And **pretend**!

❧ 34 ❧

Pretending to the Family

Vinetta looked in briefly on Sir Magnus as she passed his door.

"Yes?" said Magnus, looking up from his manuscript.

"Nothing," said Vinetta. "Just wondered if you were all right."

"Of course I'm all right," said the old man. "What do you expect me to be? All wrong?"

Vinetta was relieved to hear his irritable voice. She had thought that everyone in the house must have heard the storm outside and the commotion in the attic. If Sir Magnus was oblivious to it, perhaps they all were. There might still be time to put things right without telling any of them.

He doesn't know that anything's happened, she thought, a sort of madness taking over her brain. Maybe none of them knows.

So Vinetta might well be the only one who knew. The spirit of Kate, acting in her, had made her aware of the statues all around the house. She had seen, as in a vision, Joshua frozen in the act of hanging up his coat at work. She alone knew all that had happened up to the time when the battle ended. And that knowledge was something she would share with no one but Joshua.

Everyone in the house was briefly seen and checked. They were, as she had hoped, innocent of all knowledge of what had happened.

When she came to the lounge, however, Vinetta was horrified at Soobie's narrow escape. She almost broke down but managed to hold on to the pretend, to shut out all thought of the battle, and concentrate her attention on Soobie. She fussed over him and insisted on repairing his singed scalp immediately. The activity helped. Within a very short time Soobie's hair was almost as good as new. The blue wool from Vinetta's workbox was slightly deeper than Soobie's own hair, possibly because, being kept in the box for years, it had not faded so much.

"It'll soon blend in," said his mother. "In a week or two, you'll not be able to tell the difference."

"I still can't figure out how it happened," said Soobie.

Vinetta said nothing but looked uncomfortable.

Pilbeam looked at her suspiciously. There was something unnatural about the expression on her mother's face. She seemed to know something about the whole sequence of events that was hidden from the rest of them.

"Where's Appleby?" Pilbeam asked, suddenly guessing that her sister might be the cause of her mother's mysterious demeanor. "I was going to look for her when I heard Soobie shout."

"Appleby's having an early night," said her mother in a quick, nervous voice. "She's having an early night. She's very tired, you see. She asked me to tell you not to disturb her because she wants to go to sleep."

"I'll just look in for a minute to say goodnight to her," said Pilbeam, very suspicious now, but with no idea what might be wrong.

"No!" said Vinetta sharply. "Don't do that! I've told you. She's not to be disturbed. How would you like it if you were very tired and someone woke you up just to say goodnight? I forbid you to do anything of the sort."

Pilbeam put an arm on her mother's shoulder.

"There's something wrong," she said. "What is it?"

When Vinetta replied she sounded as ill-natured as ever Appleby had been.

"There's nothing wrong," she shouted. "Just leave her alone. She has problems. We all have problems. The trouble with you, Pilbeam, is that you don't know how to mind your own business."

Pilbeam was staggered. Never in living or unliving memory had she heard her mother speak like that. The strain of being shut in must be telling on all of them, even Vinetta, whom her daughter had always looked upon as the backbone of the family.

"I think," said Pilbeam gently, "that perhaps we should all have an early night."

She nodded a warning to Soobie, kissed her mother on the cheek, and went off to bed.

"You would tell *me* if Appleby had run away again?" said Soobie, when he and his mother were alone. "That's not what's wrong, is it?"

"No," said Vinetta wearily. "I think Pilbeam's right. We all need a good night's sleep. Things will seem different in the morning. You should go to bed now, too."

When at last she was alone, Vinetta returned to the

kitchen and, late though it was, she swept up the pieces of the earthenware bowl. The others must not see evidence of any strange occurrence. The bowl was very old, but she knew she would be able to buy one nearly identical at the Market. The fashion in earthenware bowls had not changed in a hundred years or more!

Tomorrow, Appleby would come down from the attic and it would be as if nothing had ever happened. It was perfectly possible, Vinetta told herself, as she emptied the broken pieces into the bin. Perfectly possible. Appleby had always been a survivor. That was a belief to cling to.

When all the chores were done, Vinetta grew more worried, not less. Her faith in Appleby's survival was forced and shallow, but that was not her only concern. She knew that it had been a very close call for all of them. And there was one member of the family she had not yet been able to check on. She no longer possessed Kate's knowledge. For half an hour Kate had been Vinetta, Vinetta had been Kate. It was the only way enough strength could be concentrated upon the great struggle. That oneness had ended when the attic door closed. Now Vinetta was just Vinetta, drained and half-crazed with worry and grief. She did not know whether Joshua had survived or not. Soobie had nearly perished. Who was to say that Joshua was safe?

35

Pretending to Joshua

At Sydenham's warehouse, Joshua finished hanging his coat on the peg. He felt stiff, as if he had been standing too long. He went a bit uneasily to his chair behind the desk, sat down, took out his pipe and pretended to light it. Then he leaned back, holding the bowl of the pipe in one hand and with his Port Vale mug clutched in the other. Think I'll have a walk round soon, he said to himself, I need the exercise.

When he went home next morning, Vinetta was standing at the door waiting for him. She had sat in the kitchen all night, polishing up a new pretend, a new and intricate pretend to meet an unheard of situation.

"I'm not late, am I?" he said, remembering fleetingly the one time when he had been late, after the rat had chewed his leg.

"No," said Vinetta, but she gave him a hug that baffled him. For he was a very undemonstrative man. He smiled down at her, laying one hand on her shoulder . . .

"You're an odd one, Vinny," he said. "I haven't been away for a month, you know."

"I've done bacon and eggs for your breakfast," said

Vinetta. "I thought you might enjoy a cooked breakfast for a change."

"I *knew* I could smell bacon," said Joshua, entering into the pretend. He went to the cloakroom, hung up his coat and then sat at the kitchen table, knife and fork working on the empty plate, jaws chewing the pretend meal with evident relish.

Vinetta sat and watched him for a while.

Then she said, "I've something to tell you, Josh."

Joshua knew the look on his wife's face and winced as he wondered what was coming next. She always told him everything, but he would often have preferred to be left in the dark. He eased his chair back from the table and prepared to listen. As the story of the attic door unfolded he became increasingly conscious that it rang false. There was something abnormal about Vinetta's voice. He could hear the strain in it, the effort to tell too much, yet somehow to keep back some essential detail—she seemed to be hiding a sharp needle in a stack of prickly hay.

"So where is Appleby now?" he said, interrupting her rambling tale.

Vinetta stopped speaking. She sat there at the table just staring at him.

"Appleby," Joshua repeated. "Where is she now? You both managed to keep the door closed. Then she appeared to go into some sort of trance. So where is she now?"

Vinetta shook her head.

"She must still be in the attic," she said. "She hasn't come down yet. If we just leave her there, she will be down sometime. She's like that. You know she is."

Joshua rose from the table.

"I think we'd better go and see her, both of us."

"Can't we just wait awhile? You know what she's like. She'll be angry, Josh. She'll come down when she's ready. I know she will."

Joshua said no more but took Vinetta by the arm and led her out of the room.

Appleby was in the rocking chair where her mother had left her but she was slumped to one side, limp as a puppet whose strings have snapped. Her green glass eyes were lusterless. On her lips was a loose pink thread. Her left arm was lying twisted across her lap, the cloth that covered it all crumpled.

Joshua lifted the arm and let it fall. He settled Appleby back in the chair and looked at her intently. Vinetta stood anxiously by him.

"She's dead, Vinny," said Joshua, putting one arm round his wife's shoulders. "You knew that, didn't you?"

"She's not, Josh. She can't be. Rag dolls don't die."

"She has ceased to live."

"For now. Just for now," said Vinetta. "She'll come to life again. Pilbeam came to life."

"That was different. Pilbeam had never lived."

"Appleby's been like this before, remember. When we gave her a bath, she was almost lifeless and spent months drying out in the cupboard."

Joshua took another look at the doll in the chair and then looked directly at Vinetta, his amber lozenge eyes full of loving pity. He gripped her hand.

"She is dead," he said in a quiet, gentle voice. "For

whatever reason, the spirit has left her. She will never live again.''

''No!'' screamed Vinetta, pulling away from him. ''No! You cannot say that. I won't let you say that.''

''Hush,'' said Joshua. ''Don't let the others hear. This must be orderly and it must be right.''

He stooped and picked Appleby up in both his arms, carrying her like a baby.

''Open the attic door wide,'' he said, ''and lead the way.''

Vinetta mutely obeyed.

Joshua carried Appleby down the attic stairs and along the hall into her own room. He laid her on the bed and sat down himself on the bedside chair. Vinetta stood near him. Suddenly, Joshua put his head in his hands and his body shook with inner sobs. Vinetta, watching him, did not know what to do.

The door opened and Pilbeam was about to enter, but seeing her parents there made her pause. Vinetta looked across at the door and waved Pilbeam away. When the door closed again, Vinetta sat down on the foot of the bed. A full hour passed before either she or Joshua moved.

Then Joshua raised his head and said, ''We'll leave her now. There's nothing we can do here.'' He spread the blankets over Appleby's body.

''I don't want to leave her, Joshua. I don't ever want to leave her,'' said Vinetta in a strange, stubborn voice. ''If she is dead, truly dead, I don't think I can go on living.''

''You must,'' said Joshua. ''You have other children, living children who need you. Appleby will never need you again.''

Vinetta gave Joshua a look of hatred.

"How can you accept her death? You are wicked even to let the thought enter your mind. She *can* live. She *will* live. And nothing you say will change that. I shall stay here with her till she comes to life."

"You can't, Vinetta. You can't, I tell you. Your duty is to the rest of the family now."

Vinetta was wretched and looking around for some sort of revenge on fate.

"Very well then," she snapped. "I will come and look after everyone, since that is what you say I'm on this earth for. But I can die too."

Joshua looked startled.

"No," said Vinetta bitterly. "I don't intend to do anything drastic. I won't rush into the street and tell the world what I am. There is more than one way of dying. I can go through the motions of living whilst I die inside. I will go round doing any work I need to do, but I will be dead. If Appleby is dead, so am I. What is left of me will be just a walking shell."

Joshua knew that now was not the time to argue, but something had to be said. Words of comfort would be empty. He did not even dare to clasp her hand.

"For now," he said firmly, "you must at least pretend to live, even if it is the hardest pretend of your life. You will have to try your best to staunch the suffering of all the others. They will need you more than ever. *They* loved Appleby too. They will need you to be practical and sensible. And so do I."

Joshua put his arm round Vinetta's shoulders and took her out of Appleby's room, closing the door behind them.

Vinetta said nothing, but offered no resistance. She let herself be taken downstairs to her own room.

"Lie down," said Joshua, "and think about what I have said. I am going to see the others now. I'll ask Hortensia to come in and see you."

❧ 36 ❧

The Confrontation

After Joshua had asked Hortensia to go to her friend, he hurried down to the breakfast-room and told his mother all that had happened. Or, at least, as much as she needed to know. The door in the attic was dangerous, and her granddaughter Appleby was dead. They went together to Appleby's room. Tulip felt more affectionate toward her in death than she ever had in life. A hard fact, but true.

"Miss Quigley is with Vinetta," said Joshua. "You must tell the children. Tell them as little as possible and make it as easy for them as you can."

"What about your father?" said Tulip. She stood by the bed, stroking the hair back from Appleby's brow. "He adores her. I don't know what this news will do to him."

"I shall see Father," said Joshua. "That is something that I must do."

*   *   *

It was late morning and the old man was snoozing again, having been awake very early, reading.

"Father," said Joshua, "wake up. Listen to me. There is something I have to tell you."

Sir Magnus tried to look as if he had not been sleeping and said tetchily, "Well, get on with it then. I haven't got all day."

In as few words as possible, Joshua told his father about the door in the attic and the death of Appleby.

Magnus was shattered. Hiding his grief under a blustering anger, he cried out, "I always knew that attic was dangerous. It should have been kept locked and bolted. You have all dragged me through hell this year, what with one thing and another. I am an old man. I shouldn't have to suffer like this."

"Vinetta is suffering," said Joshua. "If you could see Vinetta, you would know what suffering really is. It is driving her mad. And I can see only one way of helping her."

"Yes?" said Magnus. "And what would that be?"

"For Vinetta's sake, for all our sakes, including yours, this siege must be over. Our troubles all began with your crazy idea that we must hide ourselves away from the neighbors. You tied my family down till they were nearly stifled. Anyone could see that there would be strife. From now on, we do things my way."

Sir Magnus groaned.

"We must do our best to return to normal," Joshua continued. "We will be extra careful and extra cautious. But we must go back to living a normal life. Otherwise

192

accepting Appleby's death and learning to live with it will be impossible. We will be trapped in grief.''

''So you want them all to come and go as they like?''

''That's right. No locked doors. No stupid restrictions. Just good guidance and common sense.''

''And if we fail?'' said Granpa, white eyebrows raised. ''If some outsider discovers our secret? Have you thought about that?''

''We'll not fail,'' said Joshua, ''as long as we stick to certain practical rules.''

''How can you be so sure?''

Joshua saw with sudden clarity the true answer to his question.

''I can't be. No one can. If we *are* found out,'' he said, ''we will just have to put up with the consequences.''

Magnus worked himself up into a frenzy.

''Burnt on a bonfire,'' he said. ''Cut up in a laboratory. Paraded in a circus. Is that what you would like your family to come to?''

''So what do *you* suggest, Father? Should we open the attic door? I have lost one child. Give me credit for having some idea of how to save the others. There was a time when I agreed with you completely. I have learned the hard way that you were wrong.''

''And what of Appleby?'' asked Magnus. ''What will happen to my granddaughter now? Are you so sure she's dead? Rag dolls don't die. Look how old I am, and I go on living.''

''There is only one way to answer to that question. I'll take you to see her, Father,'' said Joshua, offering an arm and placing a walking-stick in the old man's hand. Sir

Magnus swung himself round and stood shakily on his two purple feet. Slowly they left the room and walked across to Appleby's door. Joshua opened it. On the bed, covered in the blankets, just as he had left her, was the body of his daughter.

Sir Magnus went up to the bed and took Appleby's dead hand in his. He slumped into the chair where Joshua had sat. For some minutes he did not speak.

"Why could it not have been me who died?" he said at length. "She was so full of life, so very full of life. And look at me—old and crippled and useless."

And he looked older than ever. He had come from his room without dressing gown or slippers. His purple feet looked monstrous, the left paler than the right because it had not had the continuous protection of the counterpane. His green checked nightshirt, flopping nearly to his ankles, looked undignified. Tulip would never have allowed him to leave his room in such disarray. Tulip would have insisted upon his proper attire, no matter what the emergency.

Joshua became conscious of his father's pathetic appearance. He gripped the older man's arm firmly but gently and took him back to his own room.

"And now everything returns to normal," he said, as he helped Sir Magnus back into bed. "I will tell the others today, and I will explain the precautions they must all take."

"Do what you like," said Magnus. "They can all do what they like. I don't care anymore."

The others were all told of Joshua's decision.

"And though we are now free to go in and out of the house again," said Joshua, "a watch must still be kept at the front window. *We* must become the nosy neighbors. That is just common sense.''

It was Miss Quigley who told the children that their mother would need their help.

''She has cared for you for years,'' she said. ''Now you must care for her. Think of her as being not well. Till she is better, I will look after the house and do the washing and the ironing. But you must all do your share. I have no intention of neglecting Googles.''

Poopie and Wimpey nodded solemnly. Pilbeam and Soobie resolved to give her all the help they could.

Within a few days, Vinetta managed to pull herself round enough to come out of her room and face everyone. They were all subdued, waiting for the first mention of Appleby. Soobie sat in his chair by the window and doubted whether life could be normal ever again without Appleby, Vinetta's lost sheep. Joshua kept careful watch, prepared to help, but ready to remain silent.

''You are all wondering what I am going to say,'' said Vinetta. She looked careworn. She had combed her black hair neatly and her lips were set in an unnatural smile, but her flecked blue eyes had no sparkle. ''I can see that you are. I have spent the last few days just thinking. It seems to me that no one can really be sure that Appleby is dead forever. Even where there appears to be no life there can still be hope. All we have to do is wait.''

''And in the meantime?'' asked Soobie, worried in case his mother should rely too heavily on a vain hope. Tulip had taken him and Pilbeam to see Appleby, to say their last good-byes. They had faced the reality of their sister's death. It had hurt deeply. It still hurt. But they knew it was a fact they would have to accept. It seemed to him dangerous that his mother should think otherwise.

"In the meantime," said Vinetta, giving him a sharp, comprehending look, "we live as we lived before."

It was a brave decision, not one she had reached easily. Later, Joshua spoke to Soobie alone.

"Try not to worry," he said. "Your mother will grieve some day, and in her grieving she will know that Appleby is really dead. But she is not ready for that yet."

Soobie gave his father a look of respect.

"You understand her," he said.

"I love her," said Joshua, and then turned away as if he felt he had said too much.

Of the secret visits Tulip paid to the room on the second floor, little need be said. The loose thread was trimmed from Appleby's lip, her long red hair was brushed smooth, and fresh pillows were placed beneath her head.

❧ 37 ❧

Watching

So the Mennyms went about their business as usual. Poopie worked with a will in the garden and restored it to orderliness. Joshua helped him whenever he had the time. Pilbeam went shopping. Vinetta went to the Market.

Miss Quigley waited patiently for the new pram they had decided should be bought to replace the old-fashioned one, but she was delighted to take Googles into the back garden and to sit and paint in the sheltered corner down by the hedge. And when Tulip needed a fresh supply of wool she made a ceremony of preparing to face the world and out she went, though she did feel a little disloyal to her husband. But even he managed to get over his sulks and his sorrow enough to employ Pilbeam as his errand-girl.

"Don't leave the house unless you are sure that the street is empty," he said. "And check with the look-out before you go."

The "look-out" was whoever was on duty at the upstairs window. It had been decided that the window immediately above the lounge, Joshua and Vinetta's bedroom window, would afford a better all-round view of the street. Vigilance was kept more rigorously than ever, from sunrise till sunset and a little beyond. Joshua had to take his daytime rest on the sofa in the dining room.

The watchers observed scenes from the sort of life they themselves would never lead, scenes most of them had never bothered to notice before.

The Richardsons at Number 2 suddenly acquired a new baby. Vinetta, taking her turn at the window, saw a smart young woman wheeling a small, modern pram out of the gate.

"That's what we need for Googles," she said to Hortensia who was keeping her company on the window-watch. They had looked at a fair number of Tulip's catalogs but had so far been unable to make up their minds as between a small pram, a carrycot on wheels and a large canopied pushchair.

Hortensia looked worried.

"I may have to wait a year or two before I take baby to the park again," she said. "Another baby in the street could make it awkward. Its mother might try to stop me to compare notes."

It was Soobie who saw the funeral.

"Someone must have died at Number 4," he said. There were many cars and flowers and mourners. It was from the *Castledean Gazette* that Miss Quigley produced the information that the deceased was Millicent Isabella Jarman, aged 78, wife of Andrew Jarman, mother of Oswald, George and Helen, and loving grandmother to all the family.

Watching made the Mennyms aware that the Jarmans were in no hurry to move. One of the sons was obviously still living at home, going to work in his car at the same time each morning. The father could be seen doing the garden, helped by a young man who might have been a grandson, or perhaps a handyman gardener.

Then, one Saturday morning in the middle of October, Wimpey was on watch when she saw the most exciting thing ever. A wedding! A big, wonderful wedding!

"Quick, quick, Mum," she shouted. "Come and look! Somebody's getting married."

Vinetta, Tulip and Pilbeam all came hurrying in. Looking out of the window, unable to resist the temptation to lift the net curtain, they saw the bride, on the arm of her father, standing at the gateway of Number 9. The couple were about to enter the wedding car which was a Rolls

Royce festooned with white satin ribbon. A photographer was taking a picture of the bride, who was Anthea Fryer, and her parents, Alec and Loretta. This album, Alec had decided, would be a work of art to treasure forever. Anthea had put her foot down very firmly when he had wanted to video the whole proceedings, but had given in over the album.

Anthea had given way to her mother's wishes over the dress. It was long and dreamy in satin and lace. It was totally out of character for an Amazon, but even Hippolyta had to submit to a stately wedding! The ceremony was to take place at St Mark's on Lower Malvern Street. That too had been a compromise. Her father wanted the Cathedral. Anthea, beginning to feel more mature already, favored a quiet, family wedding without any fuss. The guest list was longer than she wanted it to be, but at least the church was small and pretty, offering comfort rather than ostentation.

"She's a beautiful bride," said Vinetta. "I didn't realize how nice-looking she was."

"All brides are beautiful," said Tulip, "and at this distance you can hardly judge."

There was always something waspish about Tulip. And Anthea *was* a beautiful bride, at any distance.

The *Castledean Gazette* came out twice a week. Miss Quigley brought home the next issue and was in the lounge trying to find an account of the wedding in Brocklehurst Grove.

"It's bound to be here somewhere," she said. She peered myopically at the print.

"Let me find it for you," said Pilbeam, and Miss Quigley, feeling embarrassed at how long it might take her to find the report, or even to be sure that there was none, was glad to hand the paper over.

Pilbeam turned the pages rapidly till she caught sight of the blurred photograph of an unrecognizable bride and groom cutting a wedding cake. Even by the *Gazette*'s standards it was indistinct.

Pilbeam read aloud the paragraphs relating to the Brocklehurst Grove wedding. The usual flat account of who, where and when ended with the information that the bride and groom would be setting up home in Huddersfield.

"It's not the other side of the world," said Soobie, "but it's far enough way to serve our purpose."

"A pity the rest of the family wouldn't move away too," said Tulip when they told her. "She might still come back and visit."

"And if she does," said Vinetta, "we will know. We must never assume that she is the only danger. The watch must still be kept."

38

Pilbeam's Birthday

The attic was now a place to be remembered, never again to be seen. The remaining material in the wicker chest would never be made up into dresses or shirts. The books, the rocking chair, and all the other jumble would be left to gather dust. And Pilbeam's mirror was left there, too. It was an oval mirror in a wooden flame and it hung on a matching stand. Pilbeam's mirror? Yes, for it was through that glass that Pilbeam had first seen her own face four years ago. At that time she had been wearing her hair in two long plaits. So had Aunt Kate made her. Pilbeam had looked at herself and immediately decided that the plaits were not to her liking.

"Do you know," she said to Wimpey, "it will be four years tomorrow since I first looked at myself in the mirror in the attic."

They were sitting in the lounge at the round table, fortunately removed from the attic when Pilbeam joined the family. They were looking at the calendar, counting the days left till Christmas. Tomorrow was the twenty-eighth of October.

"St. Jude's day," said Pilbeam. "Patron saint of lost causes."

Wimpey ignored an allusion she did not understand, but came up with a different idea.

"Why don't we call it your birthday?" she said. "You and Soobie could have a party."

Till then, Appleby had been the only member of the family to celebrate her birthday. The younger twins had a "birthday" that for some unknown reason coincided with Christmas. The grown-ups were too old for birthdays. And as for Soobie, he as ever was unwilling to be part of any elaborate pretend.

Pilbeam smiled at Wimpey's words.

"I can't imagine Soobie celebrating a birthday or anything else. Still, the lost causes bit might appeal to him."

"Well, you can have the party," said Wimpey, "and Soobie can have Saint Jude."

Then, as an afterthought, she added, "And you can both be seventeen. I don't like the sound of eighteen at all. I never did. Appleby hates you to be eighteen."

Wimpey thought of her sister as being still alive though hidden in the bedroom she must never enter. The pretend was not yet over. What else could she think?

Pilbeam sighed. Any reference to Appleby hurt deeply. But Pilbeam loved Wimpey too much to give way to grief in front of her. She would not, however, agree to have a party, but to please Wimpey she promised to call the next day her birthday and to take a year off her age. It made little difference. She had added two years on, now she took one year off. Soobie would be asked to do the same.

In a mood as blue as his face, Soobie agreed to be seventeen and to accept St. Jude as a patron. To his way of thinking, nothing good had happened for a long time and nothing good seemed likely to happen. Theirs was doomed to be a hopeless case.

But the very next day, something potentially good *did* happen. Soobie was sitting at the lounge window when he saw a huge furniture van pass the front gate. It turned the corner, passed Number 7, then Number 8, and drew to a halt at Number 9. This had to be interesting. The daughter was married. Were the parents leaving too? Soobie, with an unwonted display of energy, went quickly up the stairs to his parents' room to get a better view. Pilbeam was there already, doing her official turn on watch.

"I think the Fryers must be moving," she said. "That can't be bad. Anthea will have no reason to return to Castledean. We can regard that as a good omen on our birthday."

The grand piano had been the last piece of furniture to arrive at Number 9. Soobie remembered it very clearly. Now it was to be the first to leave. Three removal men took enormous pains to put the instrument into the van. The whole job took them all of an hour and a half.

"I wonder when the rest of their furniture will be going?" said Pilbeam as the van drew away.

"They might just have got rid of the piano," said Soobie. "It could be Anthea's piano being sent to Huddersfield. The parents may not be leaving at all."

In the past weeks, the Mennyms had seen Loretta Fryer drifting round her garden, weeding the borders and pruning the roses. They had seen her jogging occasionally in a bright pink tracksuit. That disturbed Soobie, but only slightly. A middle-aged woman was not likely to go jogging late at night in the middle of winter. And Soobie had already decided not to risk jogging again before the end of November.

Alec was rather more menacing than his wife. He carried binoculars round his neck and kept picking them up to look at the birds. So far as they could tell, he was not directly nosy, but he had been seen talking to the man from Number 3, and he had actually given a lift to the older Jarman one day, after the son had gone off to work.

"Ours is a lost cause," said Soobie to Pilbeam when St. Jude was mentioned. "Do you realize that? People are becoming more and more inquisitive. They seem to think they have some sort of right to know everybody's business. You just have to look at the newspapers. There is no privacy anymore. Computers are taking over the world. They can relate facts in ways that no human can. We may not be able to confuse them for much longer. As a family, we just don't add up."

"Don't talk like that," said Wimpey, not fully understanding but knowing that her brother's words were pessimistic. "It's your birthday. You're seventeen again. The siege is over and we can all be happy."

"Yes," said Pilbeam with determination, though she understood only too well what Soobie meant, "we can. Let's go down to the lounge and have a birthday game of charades. Let's play music. Let's talk and laugh. That's what birthdays are for, aren't they?"

Soobie recognized the traces of desperation in her brittle voice and decided once more that sometimes pretends are a necessity. If we don't keep on pretending, he thought, we might not survive. It was a doctrine difficult to accept but impossible to ignore.

So they did have a party of sorts and as the afternoon went on they even became noisy and happy as if no threat loomed over them and they even managed to forget that Appleby was not there. Soobie worked harder at being happy than any of them. The older members of the family joined in. And Miss Quigley, bringing Googles to enjoy the fun, conjured up another talent—no, not a rabbit out of a hat—a sketch pad and pastels with which she drew portraits of all of them as they played. Then she pleased Poopie and Wimpey by sketching Disneyland characters, and letting the youngsters have turns at drawing too.

"That's *very good*," she said when Wimpey drew a teddybear. And she admired Poopie's graceful airplane.

Tulip sat knitting and looking unusually benign. No one is ever too old to learn. The process is just a little bit more difficult as one grows older.

"We could do with more days like this," said Vinetta. "It seems such a long time since my children were happy."

Vinetta was no longer pretending. That phase had passed. She had finally accepted the reality of her daughter's death and was coming gradually to believe in life again. Her grief for Appleby was something only Joshua had been allowed to share. It was as he had foretold. One day Vinetta had suddenly collapsed in his arms and sobbed out the pain of a broken heart. Only then did she begin to understand that to remember her lost daughter, without any desperate pretending, was in some way a celebration of Appleby's own life. The healing was slow, very slow, but sure.

❦ 39 ❦

The Last Chapter

Despite the lull, there was still no real peace of mind. The Fryers had become a symbol. Till they had gone from the street completely, the watch must be maintained, the feeling of unease must be nurtured so that danger would not have a chance to creep up on them unawares. Yet what happened next was totally unexpected.

Early one November morning, a furniture van drew up at the gate of Number 5 Brocklehurst Grove. The removers got out, opened the double gates, signaled to the driver who backed into the Mennyms' drive. It was eight-thirty in the morning. The workers had arrived on site, they had lowered the van's tailboard and were ready to begin. Then, in accordance with the custom of the company, the four of them settled down in the back of the van and ate their breakfast.

Granpa Mennym, hearing the unusual noise outside, carefully placed his lap-desk on the bedside cabinet and eased himself over to the side of his bed nearest to the window. He could just reach the net curtain. He raised it and was horrified at what he saw.

"Tulip!" he shouted. "Tulip!"

But Tulip was two floors down in the breakfast-room at the back of the house.

Vinetta, putting clothes away in the airing cupboard on the first floor, heard the old man's voice and hurried up to see him.

"It's happened," said Magnus as she entered the room. "They've found out about us and they're coming to take us away."

Vinetta looked out of the window, saw the van, and could think of no better explanation than her father-in-law's. Who had betrayed them? What should they do?

"We'll fight," said Magnus, grabbing his walking-stick. "We won't give in easily. Get the others. Tell them to be prepared."

Vinetta hesitated, wondering if it was safe to leave Magnus in this state. Then she hurried down to the dining room where Joshua was already lying asleep on the sofa.

"Josh," she said. "I think you'd better wake up. There's a big van in the front drive and we don't know what it's there for."

"Mmm," said Joshua as he turned to make himself more comfortable.

"Josh," said Vinetta more emphatically. "Wake up. Can't you hear what I'm telling you?"

Soobie had just come down from his bedroom. He went into the lounge and sat in his usual seat by the window, picked up the newspaper he had left there the night before and glanced out of the ... What is *that?* He jumped up from his chair and drew closer to the net curtain. Clearly identified now, the object blocking his view was a very big furniture van and it was parked in the drive.

"Mother!" he called. "Granny!"

Tulip came from the breakfast-room. She followed Soobie's horrified gaze.

"Why on earth is that there?" she said. "I wonder what they think they're doing."

Vinetta and Joshua came in behind her.

"Magnus thinks they have been sent here to take us away."

Poopie had the room next to his parents. It too faced the front. He got out of bed and looked out of his window. What he saw made him come dashing down the stairs, telling them all very noisily what they already knew.

"There's a van outside," he said, "and it's parked in our path."

Pilbeam, still in her dressing gown, came into the lounge. The commotion had roused her. Morning tiredness hung about her. In the deep of the night, she would lie awake wishing that Appleby would burst in and be cheeky, tell lies, do anything, but live again. So morning often found Pilbeam more ready for sleep than for rising. She saw the van in the driveway outside the window and was bewildered.

Miss Quigley was sitting in the day nursery in her big armchair. Its back was to the window and Miss Quigley was busy changing Googles into her day clothes. Whatever the noise in the lounge was about would have to wait. The nanny had very strict priorities. Baby first, anything else later.

In the van, the men had finished their first break of the day and prepared for the job ahead.

"Come on then," said Alfie Cave. "It's time we got started."

"It's a wonder nobody's come out yet. They're usually quick off the mark when they see the van," said Ted the driver.

"Mebbe they've slept in," said George, the youngest member of the crew.

"Well," said Alfie, "it's nine o'clock. We can't hang around waiting. If they're still asleep, too bad. Just watch me wake them up!"

He went to the door and pressed hard on the bell once, twice, three times. Then he waited.

Inside the house, the Mennyms in the lounge had decided that no one should answer the door. Obviously that would not be the end of the matter, but answering the door would certainly be the wrong thing to do, whatever the right thing was. They tried to stay calm.

"Mebbe the bell's not working," said George, after a minute had passed.

Alfie knocked vigorously on the rapper.

Inside the lounge, the Mennyms began to be seriously worried. Upstairs, Granpa, feeling very old and frail, trembled in his bed. Miss Quigley looked round at the window, saw the men outside the front door and shrank back in her big armchair, cuddling Googles for comfort.

Wimpey, holding her American doll, came running down the stairs. Vinetta heard her, dashed out into the hall and pulled her into the lounge.

"What's that knocking?" said Wimpey quite loudly.

Vinetta said, "Sh . . . we must be very quiet. There are some people outside trying to get in."

"My-name-is-Polly," said the doll. "What-is-your-name?"

"Shh," said Vinetta again.

"I couldn't help it, Mum," whispered Wimpey and she nursed Polly close to her chest to make sure that the noise wouldn't happen again.

"I wonder what the devil they're up to?" said Alfie. "They definitely said November the tenth. We don't make mistakes about things like that."

He banged on the door panel with his fist.

Inside, the Mennyms quaked with fear. Would these strangers break the door down and burst in? Wimpey clung to her mother.

"Unless there's nobody here. They might just be leaving us to get on with the job. I wonder if they've left the keys at the office?" said Freddie Topham. "It would be like that Jean to forget them."

"Nobody's ever left keys before, not in my time," said Alfie. "They're too worried in case anything goes wrong."

Alfie looked at the name, address and date on the work-sheet, came close to the door again, raised the letter-box and peered in. The lobby and the hall beyond were in near darkness. Alfie strained to see any sign of life.

"There's not even a crate in sight," he called back over his shoulder. "Sammy Little said he left eleven crates here yesterday."

Inside the house, the Mennyms heard Alfie's words and were petrified. Eleven crates? Eleven rag dolls. What were they planning to do? Where were they planning to take them? The Mennyms looked at one another and scarcely dared to breathe.

Alfie looked down at the worksheet again. Then he shouted up at the window, ''Mr. Fryer, Mrs. Fryer, are you there?''

Then the Mennyms suddenly knew what had happened. The van had come to the wrong address. But there was no way they could tell the removal men this vital fact. They sat still and waited.

The men outside were just deciding to ''try round the back'' when a voice called to them and feet could be heard pounding the quiet morning pavement.

Alec Fryer was running toward the Mennym house.

''Hey,'' he said, beckoning to the men as he edged past the van in the drive. ''What do you think you're up to? Acropolis Removers?''

''That's us,'' said Alfie.

''You were supposed to be at my house half an hour ago.''

''Mr. Fryer?''

''That's the name,'' said Alec, exasperated.

''Well, where's the keys then?'' said Alfie, still not grasping what had happened.

''Good grief, man,'' said Alec, ''do you not know what you've done? You've come to the wrong house. Did the people in there not tell you?''

Alec nodded toward Number 5's door.

''No answer,'' said Alfie. ''It says Number 5 on the sheet. We're not mind readers.''

''Well, try to be lip-readers,'' said Alec angrily. ''Number 9. That's where you should be. Get into that van and move it along to my house . . . now.''

"It's not our mistake," said Alfie. "We only go by what's on the sheet."

The Mennyms gave a corporate sigh of relief as the van left their driveway. From upstairs and downstairs, they watched it being loaded with all the goods and chattels from Number 9.

Then the Acropolis pantechnicon was driven away. The Mennyms watched it rounding the corner out of sight as if it were the proverbial load of hay.

"I think," said Vinetta, "that we have been given another chance, another lease of life." She straightened the net curtain and came away from the window.

"But what is life?" said Soobie.

"Life is sweet," said Vinetta. "That is all we need to know."

Read All the Stories by
Beverly Cleary

- ☐ **HENRY HUGGINS**
  70912-0 ($4.50 US/ $5.99 Can)
- ☐ **HENRY AND BEEZUS**
  70914-7 ($4.50 US/ $5.99 Can)
- ☐ **HENRY AND THE CLUBHOUSE**
  70915-5 ($4.50 US/ $6.50 Can)
- ☐ **ELLEN TEBBITS**
  70913-9 ($4.50 US/ $5.99 Can)
- ☐ **HENRY AND RIBSY**
  70917-1 ($4.50 US/ $5.99 Can)
- ☐ **BEEZUS AND RAMONA**
  70918-X ($4.50 US/ $6.50 Can)
- ☐ **RAMONA AND HER FATHER**
  70916-3 ($4.50 US/ $6.50 Can)
- ☐ **MITCH AND AMY**
  70925-2 ($4.50 US/ $5.99 Can)
- ☐ **RUNAWAY RALPH**
  70953-8 ($4.50 US/ $5.99 Can)
- ☐ **RAMONA QUIMBY, AGE 8**
  70956-2 ($4.50 US/ $5.99 Can)
- ☐ **RIBSY**
  70955-4 ($4.50 US/ $5.99 Can)
- ☐ **STRIDER**
  71236-9 ($4.50 US/ $5.99 Can)
- ☐ **HENRY AND THE PAPER ROUTE**
  70921-X ($4.50 US/ $6.50 Can)
- ☐ **RAMONA AND HER MOTHER**
  70952-X ($4.50 US/ $5.99 Can)
- ☐ **OTIS SPOFFORD**
  70919-8 ($4.50 US/ $5.99 Can)
- ☐ **THE MOUSE AND THE MOTORCYCLE**
  70924-4 ($4.50 US/ $5.99 Can)
- ☐ **SOCKS**
  70926-0 ($4.50 US/ $5.99 Can)
- ☐ **EMILY'S RUNAWAY IMAGINATION**
  70923-6 ($4.50 US/ $5.99 Can)
- ☐ **MUGGIE MAGGIE**
  71087-0 ($4.50 US/ $5.99 Can)
- ☐ **RAMONA THE PEST**
  70954-6 ($4.50 US/ $5.99 Can)
- ☐ **RALPH S. MOUSE**
  70957-0 ($4.50 US/ $5.99 Can)
- ☐ **DEAR MR. HENSHAW**
  70958-9 ($4.50 US/ $5.99 Can)
- ☐ **RAMONA THE BRAVE**
  70959-7 ($4.50 US/ $5.99 Can)

☐ **RAMONA FOREVER**
70960-6 ($4.50 US/ $5.99 Can)
